Nettie's JOURNEY

Nettie's JOURNEY

ADELE DUECK

COTEAU BOOKS FOR KIDS

FROM MANY PEOPLES

Edited by Barbara Sapergia.
Cover photo: "Girl sitting in chair reading book" by Whit Preston/Getty Images.
Cover montage and design by Duncan Campbell.
Book design by Karen Steadman.
Printed and bound in Canada by Gauvin Press.

Library and Archives Canada Cataloguing in Publication

Dueck, Adele, 1955–
Nettie's journey / Adele Dueck.
(From many peoples)

ISBN 1-55050-322-7

1. Mennonites—Juvenile fiction. 2. World War, 1914-1918—Ukraine—Juvenile fiction. 3. Soviet Union—History—Revolution, 1917-1921—Juvenile fiction. I. Title. II. Series.

PS8557.U28127N48 2005   jC813'.54
C2005-904902-2

10 9 8 7 6 5 4 3 2 1

2517 Victoria Avenue
Regina, Saskatchewan
Canada   S4P 0T2

Available in Canada & the US from
Fitzhenry & Whiteside
195 Allstate Parkway
Markham, ON,   L3R 4T8

The publisher gratefully acknowledges the financial support of its publishing program by: the Saskatchewan Arts Board, the Canada Council for the Arts, the Government of Canada through the Book Publishing Industry Development Program (BPIDP), the City of Regina Arts Commission, the Saskatchewan Cultural Industries Development Fund, Saskatchewan Culture Youth and Recreation, SaskCulture Inc., Saskatchewan Centennial 2005, Saskatchewan Lotteries, and the Lavonne Black memorial Fund.

To Nettie Dueck,
my model and inspiration
— ADELE DUECK

This book, and the rest of the
From Many Peoples *series*
is dedicated to the memory of LaVonne Black.
(See page 206)

PROLOGUE

Lisa pulled on the edge of the spongy lump of dough and pressed it into the centre with the heel of her hand. She rotated the dough and did it again.

Her grandmother watched approvingly from the chair at her side. "That looks good," Nettie said. "Now just grease the top of it with butter, then cover the bowl with a towel and we'll let it rise."

"Did you make buns like these when you lived in Russia?" asked Lisa as she followed her grandmother's instructions.

"They were much the same," said Nettie. "Of course, they were always *tweiback.*"

"Tweiback?" repeated Lisa. "What's that?"

"Double buns," said Nettie. "There was one big bun on the bottom and a littler one on top. When my mother or sisters made them, the little bun always stayed where it belonged." She laughed softly. "I was younger and not so careful. My *tweibacks* usually slid off in the oven!"

"Tell me more about when you were young," said Lisa. She washed the bun dough off her hands and pulled up a chair beside her grandmother. "What was it like in Russia? Why did you leave? Why did you come to Saskatchewan? How old were you when you came here?"

"So many questions," said Nettie. She smiled at Lisa. "The last one's the easiest. It was 1923. I was just a bit older than you. Fourteen. We travelled by train and ship and train again, and ended up just across the Saskatchewan River at Herbert."

"And..." Lisa looked expectantly at her grandmother.

"Why did we leave?" Nettie shook her head slowly. "It's such a long story. Don't you have something more fun to do than sit here listening to an old lady? Didn't your mother say you were thinking of going shopping with one of your friends?"

"I told Katelyn I couldn't come," said Lisa. "I was hoping you'd tell me more about when you were young."

A truck rumbled through the yard and Nettie smiled as she listened. "Well, if you really want to hear it," she said. "But let's sit outside in the shade. We can watch your mother and your sister bring the wheat into the granaries while we talk." She reached for her cane and rose unsteadily to her feet. "And don't say I didn't warn you. It's a long story."

"That's okay," said Lisa. She held the door open as her grandmother stepped out into the sunshine. "We've got lots of time while we wait for the buns to rise."

CHAPTER 1

Gruenfeld, Ukraine, August 30, 1916. Liese and Peter's wedding day. Liese gave me a book to write in.

Nettie lay on the bed and watched her sister brush her wavy golden hair.

"Why is the wedding at Peter's place?" she asked, twirling one of her long dark braids. "I want the wedding in our house."

Liese smiled. "Our house is too small, and so is our barn," she said. "There wouldn't be room for all the people."

"Is today your wedding day?" asked Nettie. Liese only nodded. "Then what was yesterday? You wore a new dress and the barn was full of people and we ate ham and *moos.*"

"That was the *poltaovent,*" said Liese. "The wedding is today. This afternoon. Soon. And my hair is not going the way it's supposed to." She smoothed the sides again and looked at herself critically in the mirror.

"Yesterday was the most fun I've ever had," said Nettie. "I liked the presents, too."

"Everyone was very kind," murmured Liese absently. "Perhaps my hair is good enough. What do you think?"

Before Nettie could reply, the door of the bedroom swung open. "Aganeta Pauls!" exclaimed their sister Sara indignantly, "I've been looking for you everywhere. You're supposed to get into your dress. It's almost time to leave. And look at your hair. I'll have to braid it again."

"I want a new dress. Liese has one."

Sara threw her hands up in the air. "You don't need a new dress. I don't even have a new dress. Hurry."

"Wait, Sara," interrupted Liese. "I want to talk to Nettie for just a moment." At Sara's frustrated look, Liese smiled. "I won't keep her long, I promise."

"I'll be waiting for you," Sara told Nettie as she hurried away.

"I have a gift for my little sister," Liese said. Nettie saw just a glimpse of a small dark object before it disappeared behind Liese's back.

"I'm going to miss you when I'm married to Peter," said Liese, bending down so her face was level with Nettie's. "And you are going to grow up without me being here with you. I want to give you something that will help you remember me all the time."

"But you're going to live in Gruenfeld, aren't you?" asked Nettie, suddenly afraid. "I can visit you."

"Yes, I'll be in the village, but it won't be the same as when we share a house. I made this for you so you will remember that I love you."

She took her hand from behind her back. In it was a small book, hand-sewn, and full of empty pages.

"This is a diary," said Liese. "You write in it about things that happen to you."

Nettie accepted the book with awe. Would she ever be able to write enough words to fill so many empty pages?

"Liese, are you ready?" It was Mama this time, bursting into the room, her large frame in her black dress filling the doorway, leaving no space for Nettie to squeeze past.

"What, little one? You're not dressed yet? Hurry, hurry, your Sunday dress is on my bed. Sara will help you."

She stepped aside so Nettie could leave. Before the door closed behind her, Nettie heard her mother say, "Oh, my dear Liese, you look so beautiful."

That's what Nettie thought too, later, as she sat with all their friends and relatives in the Peters' barn. Everyone who had a bench had lent it, till the barn was filled with rows and rows of benches. With no backs, they were uncomfortable to sit on, but it seemed to Nettie that she was the only one who thought so. She looked sideways at her brother Jacob. Well, perhaps he was uncomfortable too. She glimpsed his feet swinging briefly before a glance from Sara caused them to still. She knew he wasn't happy to be sitting with the women. He thought he was old enough to sit on the other side of the room with the men. Nettie sighed soundlessly, and tried to identify the people in front of her by their backs.

Liese and Peter were here, of course, right at the front in their chairs decorated with vines and leaves. Liese wore a beautiful white dress that she and Mama had made. Her hair was swept up smoothly and topped with a crown of myrtle leaves that held her veil in place. Peter looked very handsome in his black suit. He had a large boutonniere, Nettie knew, though she couldn't see it from behind.

Mama and Papa and Peter's parents, Mr. and Mrs. Peter Peters, Senior, were sitting in the front. Grandma and Grandpa Pauls were there too. This was a very special occasion, indeed, for them to travel so far. There were several aunts and uncles as well, many of whom Nettie hardly knew. One of them was Aunt Nettie, Mama's sister, after whom Nettie was named. Nettie saw her sitting a couple rows ahead.

The gift-giving party the day before had been more fun, Nettie thought. It was in this barn too. Decorated with branches and vines of green leaves along with flowers from Sara's garden, the barn didn't look as if anyone had ever threshed grain or stored feed in it. All their close friends and relatives had shared a meal and then given gifts to Liese and Peter: beautiful dishes, handmade quilts, embroidered tea towels. Nettie was especially impressed with how many down-filled pillows they'd received. More than the whole Pauls family owned, she was sure.

After the gifts were admired, friends of Peter and Liese presented a program with skits that made everyone laugh, and poems written especially for them.

Nettie stayed up much later than usual. It had been a very special day.

Today was supposed to be more special, Nettie knew, because today Liese and Peter would become Mr. and Mrs. Peter Peters. But why did the service last so long? The only relief from the long sermons was the opportunity to sing hymns between speakers. Everyone sang together, but in parts. Nettie listened carefully to Sara, following her lead as best she could.

When yet another pastor took his place at the front, Nettie peeked quickly over her shoulder. Near the back wall were the tables of food for after the ceremony. There were baskets of *tweiback,* dozens of *tweiback,* maybe even hundreds of *tweiback.* It would be terrible to run out of these special two-layered rolls, so Mama and the aunts had baked all day yesterday. Mama had even made extra dough, which she'd sent with Abram and Jacob to the neighbour ladies to bake. She wanted to be sure there were enough buns to feed all the people. Along with the *tweiback,* there was butter and jam and coffee and sugar cubes.

Nettie wanted to eat right now. Dinner had been a hurried meal. Papa had barely asked the blessing before Mama was urging everyone to finish eating so she could tidy up. In the end, Aunt Nettie and Sara did the dishes, Mama hurrying off to help Liese with her dress.

Nettie felt a gentle tug on her arm. The service was finally done. Everyone stood to greet the newly married couple. Almost everyone. Nettie glanced hungrily over her shoulder and saw her cousin Gerhard sneak one of the buns out of a *tweiback* basket. And there was her brother Abram, looking so tall and dignified, until Nettie realized he was sucking on a sugar cube. With a happy sigh, Nettie joined her cousins Tina and Katie, who were waiting to wish Peter and Liese well.

While she waited, Nettie listened to bits of conversation going on around her.

"Johann Schroeder and Tina Penner will be getting married next week," said a nearby lady.

"And Cornie Wall and Anna Kornelson's wedding is next month," replied her friend.

The two ladies laughed together. "These young people must think we have nothing to do but bake *tweiback* and go to weddings," said one of them. Nettie silently agreed. What else was there to do, after all?

As the two ladies moved away to speak to her mama, Nettie heard a couple of men talking.

"Did you hear that some of our boys from Molotschna were badly injured?"

Nettie froze where she stood.

"No," the other man replied. "What happened? An accident?"

"They were Red Cross workers in Galicia. They were shelled while taking injured soldiers to the train."

"I guess it's going to happen. The Germans aren't checking to be sure that everyone they hit is carrying a gun."

Nettie pressed her hands against her cheeks, listening.

"The way I hear it, not all the Russian soldiers are carrying guns either. I don't understand what the government is doing. Not enough food, not enough uniforms, not enough guns. What way is that to treat soldiers? I don't believe in fighting, but if they are going to do it, they should do it right."

Nettie's frightened thoughts were interrupted by a tug on her arm. "Nettie, are you dreaming?" asked her cousin Tina, her round face filled with laughter. "We're almost to the front of the line and you're still here."

"No, no, of course not," said Nettie, looking around in surprise. "I'm coming." She shoved the thoughts of war away and brought herself back to the moment. Her sister was married, people were eating and visiting. Soon there would be singing and maybe the children would play games outside.

There was nothing quite so special as a wedding.

CHAPTER 2

September 25, 1916. Everyone is gone but Papa, Mama, Jacob, and me. We are drying apples and pears and plums. We are finished making all the watermelon syrup.

The house was quiet. Nettie helped her mother and thought about her absent family. Liese and Peter were on bridal visits to relatives who'd been unable to attend the wedding. They would be gone a long time.

Abram was at the Business School in Berdiansk. It was so far away he would not even be home for Christmas. Sara was closer, at the girls' school in Chortitza.

This left just Jacob and Nettie to go with Papa, every day but Sunday, out of the teacherage and into the attached schoolhouse. Papa and Jacob went into the first room, Nettie to the other room where Miss Doerksen taught.

Each day after school Jacob rushed through the connecting door out of the schoolroom and back into their house. He changed swiftly into his work pants, filled his pockets with roasted buns, and was gone before Papa bid all his students goodbye.

Jacob worked for Isaac Toews, helping with harvest. Though Nettie didn't think he was nearly old enough to work like a man, Papa and Mama were proud of Jacob.

"Isaac likes the way he handles the horses," Papa told Mama soon after Jacob started working. "He's as good as a man, though he's only twelve."

Nettie wished there was something she could do so Papa would praise her too. Working with horses and earning money seemed much more important than fetching for Mama, or sitting at the table with a board and a knife cutting apples.

It was fall and there were apples to dry. So many apples, surely they would never eat them all. And when Mama said they had dried enough apples, they cut up plums and pears! Fortunately, Nettie was at school most of the day, or she would have spent even more hours cutting fruit.

Nettie liked going to school. She liked her teacher, and playing with the other students. The difficult part was learning new languages. The words Nettie learned to write at school were not the same words she spoke every day at home. When she talked to Mama or visited with her friend Lena at the mill, they always spoke

Plautdietsch, or Low German. In school and in church, the language was High German. That was the language she wrote in her new diary.

"Why can't I write the words we say all the time?" she asked her papa one Sunday. They never cut up fruit to dry on Sunday. Papa laughed and said, "You ask too many questions. That's just the way it is. Our *Plautdietsch* is not a written language. No one knows how to spell the words. We write in German just like the people in Germany do, and the Mennonites in America, and the German Lutherans in the village down the road. We can all read the same Bible and study the same books and we can do business with each other." But then he stopped smiling and his face grew grim. "Or at least we used to."

"What do you mean, Papa? We used to? Don't those people speak German anymore?"

Papa didn't say anything for a moment. Then he lowered himself to the *schloapbenjk,* pulling Nettie down beside him..

"It's like this," he began. But then he was silent for a long time, as if he didn't know what to say. Nettie ran her hand over the smooth wood of the sleeping bench and waited for Papa to speak.

"You know about the war, don't you?" he asked, starting again.

"Yes," said Nettie, trying to remember what she'd heard. "Russia is fighting against Germany and Wilhelm

Suderman and David Gerbrandt had to go and help the injured soldiers."

"That's right," said Papa. "Russia is fighting against Germany, so now the Russian people think everyone who speaks German is fighting against Russia."

"But how can that be?" asked Nettie. "I speak German and I'm not fighting against Russia."

"But the people in Moscow don't know that," said her father, and he sighed. "Even some of the people around here don't know that."

"Not the Mennonites!"

"No, no, of course not, but the peasants. You know some of them refuse to work for the Mennonites now. And the government made a law that no one is allowed to speak German in public."

"But the minister still speaks German. Will he have to go to jail? And you speak German in school."

"Yes," agreed her father. "But not as much as before. And of course you are learning Russian as well."

Nettie nodded her head sadly. Yes, she was learning Russian as well. Sometimes she didn't know what to write in her diary. She thought in *Plautdietsch*, she was learning to write German, which she could mostly understand, but this Russian.... She only spoke Russian in school, Mama didn't speak it at all. Abram, now, he could speak Russian almost as well as Papa, because he was away at school. He met many people and even traveled on the train.

"But the war isn't coming here, is it?" asked Nettie suddenly.

Papa laughed and Nettie's heart lifted. "No, little one, the war is a long way from this corner of Ukraine. They are fighting in the west and in Europe. They are not going to fight here." And Papa gave her a big hug before he stood up.

The war is not coming here, Nettie repeated to herself. Papa had said that, so it must be true. But what about people going to the war? What about Abram, who was already as tall as Papa, though he was only sixteen years old? What if the government decided he needed to go to war? He wouldn't carry a gun, of course, Mennonites did not carry guns. But they were close to guns. They helped injured soldiers. They worked on trains that went up to the battlefields. And sometimes, thought Nettie, remembering the men talking at the wedding, sometimes they got hurt.

But no, Nettie told herself, sixteen wasn't a man yet. They wouldn't take Abram to war.

"Papa?" she whispered. Papa leaned against the side of the big central stove, his head bent over a book. In the winter he sat there enjoying the heat from the day's baking. On this warm autumn day, when there'd been no fire, it was a cool place to sit.

"Papa?" she whispered again. She didn't want to interrupt his reading, but what if he wasn't reading? Maybe he was just thinking and would hear her voice.

But Papa's head didn't lift. He turned the page and continued to read. Nettie said to herself, *Abram won't go to war.* She said it several times. After a while it seemed that it must be true.

CHAPTER 3

March 18, 1917. Today I played at the mill with Lena. Her father said the Czar is gone.

Nettie would have visited Lena at the mill every day if Mama had let her. The Remples' house was so elegant. It was bigger than the teacherage, with beautifully carved furniture. Lena had her own bedroom; her younger brothers had a room they shared. Lena's mother didn't make the meals; they had two servant girls all the time. Sometimes Nettie's mother had a servant too, but just when she was very busy or when one of the babies was sick.

There had been one baby that Nettie could remember, and another that Sara had told her about. They both died when they were very young. Nettie wished she had a sister or even a brother close to her age, but there was no one. Jacob was closest, but he thought he was a man, too old to play.

Nettie liked it best when Mrs. Remple let her and Lena play with Lena's special dolls. They had china heads and lace dresses and were stored in the china cabinet in the front room where children were not usually allowed to play. Lena begged her mother for permission to play there so her brothers couldn't bother them.

"When it's summer you may go swimming in our pool," Lena told her doll as she walked her along the border of the rug in the front room. "She can't really," Lena whispered to Nettie, "because it will spoil her, but by summer she'll forget!"

"We will walk in the sunshine in the summer," Nettie told the doll she held. She didn't want to lie, not even to a doll. But *I* will swim in Lena's pool, she thought. She looked outside where the bare branches of the mulberry bushes surrounded the houses and bits of snow still lay on the north sides of the buildings. As she looked she saw a wagon approach the house from the street and pull up in front of the barn.

"Your father is home," she told Lena.

"My father!" Lena squealed, "but we didn't expect him for three more days." She rushed over to the soft plush sofa and threw herself across it to see better out of the window. "How did he get here?" she asked. "Isaac Woelk is taking the carriage to meet the train on Friday. Papa can't be here today."

The girls saw Mr. Remple disappear into the house, his arms full of packages. "Let's see what Papa brought from Odessa," exclaimed Lena. "Come, Nettie." Lena plopped her doll on the sofa and ran for the door. Nettie picked the doll up, and after straightening her skirt, placed both dolls against a cushion in the corner of the sofa.

When she stepped into the hall, she saw Mr. Remple, still holding the packages, laughing down at his young sons. Gustav was trying to climb his father like a tree. Peter sat on his father's foot, both arms wrapped tightly around his leg. Lena danced eagerly around him, reaching for a parcel.

Nettie hung back in the doorway, wondering if she should go home.

Mrs. Remple came into the hall. "Herman, how can you be here?"

"Everything in Odessa was in an uproar," said Mr. Remple. He patted the top of Gustav's head. Gustav grabbed at his hand for support. "Everything is changed. The trains were not selling tickets. People were riding for free. I just got on the train and found a seat. When I got to Chortitza, I saw Isaac with the ladder wagon, so I came home with him."

"You came in the wagon!" exclaimed Mrs. Remple.

"It doesn't matter," said Mr. Remple. He waved his arms in the air and Gustav tumbled to the floor. "Czar Nicholas," Mr. Remple began, not seeming to notice Gustav lying on the floor, wildly kicking his legs, "he's not the czar anymore." He handed Lena a small package, which she eagerly unwrapped. The boys turned their attention from their father to Lena.

"What do you mean?" asked Lena's mother. "How can the Czar not be the czar?"

"When he quits...resigns...abdicates," said Mr. Remple. "The workers in the cities have rebelled. Nicholas finally understood he could not go on being our leader, so he quit."

"Who is the czar now?" asked his wife, confused.

"There is no czar." Mr. Remple glanced down at the children. Lena was dividing the candy into three piles. "There's a new government now," he went on. "This could be a very good thing for us, my dear. I worried that I would have to sell the mill and our fields, but now with this new government I don't believe those laws will be enforced. We can go on with our life just as in the past. It is a great day for Russia." He laughed as he handed his wife one of the parcels. "A great day!"

Later Nettie sucked on a Lobster candy as she walked home. Lena had given her one of the candies from her father. It was wrapped in a paper with a picture of a lobster on it, but Nettie was sure it tasted better than any lobster anyone had ever eaten. It was hard and sweet, but Lena told her the centre would be soft and creamy.

Nettie sat on the bench outside their house till the candy had completely melted away, then looked for her father.

She found him walking home from a visit with the other men at the store. She thought his face grew paler when she asked about the czar, but he patted her head and smiled. "When we get a newspaper from Moscow, we'll know more," he said. "Maybe then we'll know what this means for the Mennonites."

CHAPTER 4

May 30, 1917. Jacob helped Isaac Toews seed his crops. I helped Mama and Papa plant both of our gardens. Sara and Abram are home from school.

There wasn't a czar in Petrograd anymore, but Nettie's life stayed the same. When the weather grew warm, Sara and Abram came home from their schools and it seemed like they had never left.

Sara started spring cleaning. Mama hadn't done it in the spring when there was no one but Nettie to help her.

Nettie helped Sara drag the mattresses outside to air in the sun. The washerwoman who came every six weeks to wash the clothes and bedding had extra work to do, with blankets and quilts to wash as well. Nettie helped Sara wash the delicate lace curtains, then Mama ironed them smooth and hung them back over the shining clean windows. Often they sang while they worked. It made the time more pleasant, but it didn't go by any faster. It was a whole week before Sara was able to spend an afternoon in the garden.

Nettie knelt beside Sara while she tended her flowers. She pulled weeds, moved plants to bare spots, and seeded new flowers that Nettie had never heard of.

"Tell me about the tulips," said Sara. "The worst thing about going away to school is missing the early spring flowers, so tell me how they looked."

"I picked some and brought them in the house," said Nettie. She touched a faded leaf that showed where a tulip used to bloom. "They grew taller than I remembered from last year. There are still yellow ones on the other side of the house."

Sara smiled at Nettie. "The place where I board in Chortitza has a hedge of lilacs around the yard. They smell so beautiful when they bloom." Nettie nodded and listened while Sara talked about school, about the friends she had made there. About the brothers of her schoolmates who sometimes picked the girls up in their wagons and took them for a drive in the country. Nettie watched Sara while she talked and thought how pretty she looked.

"Nettie, look. This violet is going to bloom soon." Sara glanced at Nettie. "What are you staring at? Do you see the bud?"

"Yes, of course," said Nettie, obediently looking down at the tiny plant Sara was showing her in the dark brown soil. "That means it really will be summer soon." She smiled at Sara and Sara smiled back at her.

Both Abram and Jacob found work with farmers for the summer. Many farmers hired Russians or Ukrainians to work for them, but lots of Mennonite boys didn't have their own land and needed work too. Isaac Toews hired Jacob again. He liked it there; he worked with Cornie and Heinrich, two of Mr. Toews's sons and Kolya, a Russian. They were all good friends, eating together and sharing the work. When he came home at night, he always had funny stories to tell.

Abram didn't talk and laugh as much as Jacob. Nettie thought he might like to go to university when he was finished at the *Kommerz Schule*. He wanted to know many things but maybe not how to make the wheat grow.

The farmer who hired Abram lived in Steinfeld. It was about seven versts north of Gruenfeld, too far for Abram to walk twice each day. Instead he slept in the Schroeders' barn and ate in the shed behind the house with the Russian workers. Some rich Mennonites thought they were better than the poor Mennonites. Nettie could tell from the little Abram said that the Schroeders were that kind of people. Abram didn't enjoy working for them, but he needed to work to help the family. Papa didn't make much money as a teacher. Soon there would be three of his children away at school. Listening to Abram and Jacob talk about working and earning money, Nettie realized it was a good thing Liese was married.

June 12, 1917. Mama let me stay at Lena's for the night. The maid came home late after the door was locked. Mrs. Remple would not let her in but made her stay in the space between the doors all night. I'm not sure if Mrs. Remple is a nice lady, but she serves very good meals.

Nettie and Lena were playing paper dolls at Lena's house when Sara came over and talked to Nettie. "You are going to stay here tonight," said Sara. "And Mrs. Remple has asked you to come for dinner tomorrow too." Nettie stared at Sara. She had never stayed the night with Lena before. She had never even asked, knowing that Mama would say it was foolishness.

"Why are you staring?" asked Sara briskly. "Mama is tired and wants to rest. You can come home tomorrow after school."

That night Nettie and Lena whispered and giggled together, curled up beneath the soft feather quilt.

"Why do you think your mama wanted you to sleep here?" Lena asked.

"You heard Sara," said Nettie airily. "She is tired."

But that made no sense, for Mama had been tired other times, and Nettie had walked very quietly, and helped make supper. This was strange. Mama seemed so strong. Nettie tried not to think about it as she cuddled with one of Lena's rag dolls.

She went home with Lena at noon the next day. They ate spring *borscht* and white bread. As the girls walked back to school, Nettie saw Papa outside with the grade fives and sixes, but she didn't have a chance to talk to him. That afternoon, Nettie found it difficult to pay attention to her teacher.

After school she rushed home. Sara was in the kitchen washing dishes. The house was quiet. "Where is Mama?" asked Nettie breathlessly. "What is happening?"

"Have some *pluma moos*," said Sara. "You must be hungry."

Nettie glanced at the big bowl of fruit soup on the table, but before she could speak, she heard a sound, a tiny cry, then Mama's low voice.

"A baby!" exclaimed Nettie. "We have a new baby!" She turned and ran towards Mama's room, paying no attention to Sara's voice urging her to walk softly.

Mama was sitting up in bed, her hair loose around her shoulders. All Nettie could see of the baby was a bundle of blankets in Mama's arms. Nettie paused at the door, awestruck at the wonder. The baby whimpered again, and Mama patted the bundle softly.

"May I see her?" asked Nettie. "What's her name?"

"Of course," said Mama. She smiled at Nettie and moved the blanket so Nettie could see the baby's face. "His name is Johann."

His name? For one brief moment Nettie was disappointed. Then she looked into the tiny round face, all red and wrinkled and sleepy looking, and it didn't matter that the baby wasn't a girl. He opened his mouth in a giant yawn. One little fist escaped from the blankets and waved in the air.

"He's sooo beautiful," breathed Nettie.

"Sit on the bed," said Mama, "and you may hold him."

Little Johann wiggled on Nettie's lap. His tiny blue eyes opened and he started to cry.

"He doesn't like me," said Nettie, struggling to hold the bundle more securely. "He's slipping away."

"I'll rescue you," said Papa. Startled, Nettie jumped and grabbed the baby more tightly. She hadn't heard Papa come in. "Johann will soon think you are the best sister in the world," he assured Nettie as he lifted the baby from her lap. "For now he likes to be held very snugly, see?"

Papa must have been right. The cries stopped and Johann's little eyes gazed solemnly around the room.

CHAPTER 5

September 10, 1917. The apples are ripe on the trees. Mama says we must dry them. I don't know why. We still have dried apples from last year.

When September came, Sara and Abram went back to their schools. This time Jacob went too. In between gardening and cooking and caring for Johann, Mama and Sara had prepared their clothes. Abram's and Sara's uniforms needed some turning and mending, but Jacob needed a new uniform. They didn't wear them at the village school.

Mama was surprised when she took freshly made butter to the store and found there was little cloth to be had.

"It's the war," the storekeeper explained. "It disrupts everything."

Mama put some money on the counter beside the butter. Then Mr. Neufeld remembered he had some cloth in the back that was just what they needed for Jacob's school clothes.

Because Papa didn't own a horse or wagon, Isaac Woelk took Abram, Jacob, and Sara in one of the mill wagons to catch the train back to school.

With Jacob gone, Nettie helped with the animals. Mama rose early each morning to milk the cows in the small barn attached to the house, while Nettie fed the hens in the shed in the backyard and collected the eggs. After Mama took the milk into the kitchen, Nettie led Blossom and Daisy out to meet the Ukrainian herdsman. He went through the village every morning, gathering all the cows. He took them to the meadow outside the village where they grazed all day, then brought them back in time for evening milking.

Liese came to the teacherage almost every day. She helped Mama boil down the watermelons into syrup and sat with Nettie as they prepared fruit for drying. She made pickles too. Often Nettie walked home with her afterwards, carrying some of the food they had prepared.

After school on warm days, Nettie and Lena played in the sand of the schoolyard. It was soft yellow sand which they shaped into houses and roads and shops. It seemed, though, that just when the sand town looked the way they wanted it to, Mama called for Nettie. "Come rock the baby," she said. Then Nettie left Lena and the carefully made shapes, knowing that by the next day someone would come along and flatten all the little buildings.

Back in the house, Nettie sat in a darkened room and rocked Johann's wooden cradle back and forth, back and forth. Nettie hated rocking the cradle, and sometimes, as Johann cried and cried, she wondered if she hated him too.

November 7, 1917. Today we butchered hogs with Remples. Lena and I helped to stir the kettle of lard as it melted. The ambulance workers are coming home.

"Is the war over?" Nettie asked her father.

He shook his head. The sun was warm though the air was cool. Papa sat on the step of the schoolhouse. Nettie sat beside him, watching the birds pick up scattered grain by the mill as they talked.

"No," he said. "They are still fighting in western Europe." Europe, thought Nettie. That was England and Germany and other countries she couldn't remember.

"Then why are the soldiers coming back?"

Papa looked surprised. "How did you know the soldiers were coming back?"

"Jakob Gerbrandt told us in school," said Nettie. "His brother David was in the ambulance service. He said the Russian soldiers stopped fighting and were just going home. There was nothing else for him to do, so he came home too."

"Yes," said Papa. His voice sounded sad. "Our new government is trying to change things inside Russia. They've forgotten our soldiers fighting in the war."

Nettie waited for Papa to say something else. When he didn't, she went back into the house and checked on Johann. When he wasn't crying, she liked to play with him. She played a counting game with his toes and they played peekaboo. Then she sang "God is So Good." Johann smiled and Nettie thought she might burst from happiness.

November 23, 1917. Visited Lena. There are bandits in Gruenfeld.

Nettie and Lena sat on the sofa looking at Lena's mother's collection of cards. They were beautiful cards with painted flowers and vines and birds in colours brighter than any Nettie had ever seen.

"This one came from my grandmother in Molotschna," said Lena. "She always sends us the prettiest cards."

Before Nettie could comment, there was a loud knocking at the front door.

Lena continued talking about the cards, but Nettie listened to the voices from the other room.

"Where is the man of the house?" demanded the unseen man at the door. His voice was harsh and angry. "We need horses. Where is he?"

"He's working." That was Mrs. Remple's voice. She sounded stern, as if she was talking to a naughty child. "We have no horses to sell."

"Oh, you will sell horses to us," said the man, and he laughed as if he'd told the funniest joke. "Where is your husband?"

"He is in Steinfeld on business," said Mrs. Remple. "The horses are pulling the carriage."

"You expect us to believe those are your only horses? A wealthy mill owner like your husband must own many horses."

By this time Lena was listening too, the colourful cards forgotten on her lap. Lena's usually pink cheeks were pale. Suddenly she reached out and grabbed Nettie's hand, clutching it tightly.

"He will be home shortly," said Mrs. Remple, her voice still firm. Nettie marvelled that she didn't sound afraid. "You may wait outside if you like, but he will tell you the same thing. We have no horses for sale."

"How kind of you. Do you hear that, friends? We may wait outside. Well, perhaps we will do just that. And perhaps we will check out the barn while we are outside, and see what horses your kind husband left at home today."

"No!" exclaimed Lena's mother. "Stay out of the barn. Just wait in the street."

But the men weren't listening. The door slammed shut before she'd finished speaking.

Lena let go of Nettie's hand and turned quickly on the sofa to look out the window, the cards falling forgotten to the floor in a splash of colour.

Nettie knelt beside Lena just in time to get a glimpse of four men. They moved out of sight, but not towards the street. They were headed for the barn.

"What are they doing?" whispered Lena. "Why are they still in our yard when Mama told them to go to the street?"

They heard someone yelling. A moment later the four men appeared leading a horse with a shiny brown coat and three white stockings. Lena gasped. "That's Papa's colt. He'll never let anyone buy him. What are they doing?"

Suddenly another man came running behind the four men. It was old Karl Guenter, one of Mr. Remple's workers. He held a long pitchfork in one hand, and yelled at the men to bring the horse back.

Two of the men kept walking with the horse. The other two turned around and pulled sabres from their belts. They pointed them at Karl.

Karl stopped suddenly, swaying slightly, leaning on the fork. One of the men yelled something Nettie couldn't make out. Karl took a step forward, lifting the fork in the air. The other man moved towards Karl, his arm with the sword stretched out in front of him. Karl's hand dropped and he took a step backwards. The men laughed and followed after the horse.

Karl stood alone in the street, watching them lead away his employer's favourite horse.

Lena's mother must have been watching too, because now she strode indignantly out of the house. Nettie could hear her words through the open door.

"Karl," she exclaimed, "why did you let them take your master's horse? Did they give you money? Give it to them and bring the horse back."

"No, missus. They didn't give me money." Karl's voice as he turned to speak to Mrs. Remple matched his dejected appearance. "They just took the horse. They said if I tried to stop them they would kill me. I said we would go to the police and report them for theft. They said, 'Fine, you do that.' Then they laughed and went away. I knew their swords were sharp. I'm an old man and they are young and strong. So I watched them take Cossack away." Even from the distance, Nettie could see the tears roll down old Karl's face.

"If only Papa would come right now," said Lena, her mouth set so Nettie thought she looked like her mother. "If he came right now, he could take another horse and chase after them. He would stop them for sure."

But Mr. Remple didn't come right away. Lena's mother went to the mill and told the men working there to find the thieves. By the time Nettie had scurried across the street to her home, the searchers were all back. No one had caught a glimpse of either the horse or the bandits.

Nettie told her family about the horse when she got home, though somehow Papa had already heard. No one said very much about it, but after the table was cleared away, Nettie saw Mama and Papa standing by the big stove that filled the centre of the house. They looked at the bricks that kept sparks from starting the floor on fire.

Nettie sat on a chair in the corner of the room and watched them. She wanted to ask what they were doing, but she knew Papa would say, "You can see what we're doing. Don't ask when you can see." So Nettie sat and watched.

It seemed as if Mama and Papa were talking to each other without saying any words. They looked at the bricks for a long time. Then they looked at each other. Papa nodded his head. Mama looked back at the floor, then she nodded her head too.

"Time for bed," Mama said suddenly, turning around. "You had too much excitement today. You need sleep."

Nettie went to bed because that's what children did when their parents told them to, but she wasn't happy. She wanted to know why Mama and Papa were staring at the floor and nodding their heads at each other.

Once in bed, she couldn't sleep. The bed was big, for it was Sara's bed too, when she was home. Tonight Nettie wiggled and turned so much, she needed the whole bed.

Nettie could hear sounds from the other room, but they weren't the sounds of Papa's pages turning or

Mama's knitting needles. They were grating sounds, chinking sounds. Sounds of metal and stone. Finally Nettie could stand it no longer. She crept out of bed and peeked into the other room.

Mama and Papa were kneeling on the floor by the stove. Bricks were piled up around them, and Mama held something in her hand. It was shaped like a brick, but it wasn't the same colour. She stretched out her arm to hand the object to Papa. Nettie realized what it was. It was the metal box in which Papa kept his important papers.

Nettie watched as the box disappeared in front of Papa. Then he picked up a brick, followed by another brick. Soon all the bricks were gone from Nettie's sight. Papa and Mama stood up, brushing the brick dust from their clothes. To Nettie, shivering in her nightdress behind the door, the space in front of the firebox looked exactly the same as it had before she went to bed. The metal box was nowhere in sight.

Soundlessly Nettie took a step backwards and scurried back to bed. She would have liked to stay longer, to see if Papa and Mama would say anything interesting, but she didn't like to think of what would happen if they caught her spying on them. She'd seen enough and her bed was invitingly warm.

The men with the sabres were in the Pauls' house now. They hadn't found a horse in the barn and had come to ask where the horses were. They couldn't find anyone in the house but Nettie. She was in her bed. One of the men pointed a sword at her and demanded she tell him where her father was. "He's taken the horses and run away?" suggested the man.

Nettie shrank back against her pillow and said, "No, no, we don't have any horses." The man didn't believe her. He came closer.

Nettie yelled, "No! No!" then she felt something cool against her forehead. She opened her eyes and Mama was there.

"What's the matter?" asked Mama. "Why are you yelling so?"

"It was the men with the swords," Nettie sobbed, clinging to her mother. "They were looking for Papa and they pointed their swords at me."

"Hush, now; it was just a dream." said Mama soothingly. "Don't worry, the bad men won't come here."

"But Mama, they went to the Remples'. That's just across the street!"

"Yes, darling. But the Remples have horses. We don't have horses. There's nothing for them to steal here."

"How will they know we don't have horses? They might think we're hiding them."

"We live by the school. Everyone knows schoolteachers are not wealthy. Don't be afraid, little one. You'll be safe here."

"Is the door latched?"

"Yes, the door is latched. Now go back to sleep." Mama hummed a hymn quietly as she stroked Nettie's hair. Nettie curled up, hugging her pillow, trying to sleep. After a while Mama went back to her own room, but Nettie lay awake and listened to the sounds the house made at night. She wondered if thieves would really know they had nothing to steal. And she wondered about the metal box that Papa had buried beneath the bricks.

CHAPTER 6

December 2, 1917. A strange day. Johann never stops crying.

The men usually stood around outside after church talking and laughing together, but today they spoke as quietly as at a funeral.

"It's the Bolsheviks," said Papa later as he and Mama walked home ahead of Nettie. "Henry Suderman said they have taken over the government. They are going to turn the whole country communist."

"What does that mean?" asked Mama. She patted Johann but looked at Papa. "What does it mean to us?"

"You remember in 1915?" asked Papa. "The czar said German-speaking people weren't allowed to own property?"

Mama nodded and so did Nettie. She often heard people talking about that unfair law. The Mennonites were relieved the law was hardly ever enforced when the government became so busy with the war.

"People say no one will be allowed to own property now," said Papa. "*No one.* Everything will belong to the government and the people will all be workers."

"No one can own property?" repeated Mama. She shrugged her shoulders. "Well, we don't own anything for them to take away."

"Maybe not," said Papa, "but other people do."

Like Lena's family, thought Nettie. If the government owned their mill, would they still live in their house? What about the farmers with their fields? How could they take away their fields?

Nettie wished Jacob was home to talk about the news. He would say more than Papa. Maybe she would understand better.

It snowed that night while they slept. When Nettie fed the chickens before school the next day, the world seemed new. Snow covered all the ground and the roofs of the buildings and even weighed down the branches of the trees. The only marks in the snow were where Papa had shovelled the school step.

February 14, 1918. Yesterday was January 31 but today is February 14 because the government changed the calendar. From now on my birthday will be July 20 instead of the 7th. Christmas will still be December 25. Why doesn't it change like my birthday? How can the government change the calendar? Papa says they changed it so we are the same as the rest of the world.

February 18, 1918. The saddest day.

Mama sat in her rocking chair holding Johann. There was no food on the table. Nettie was surprised. Mama always had dinner ready for them. She started to say something, then realized that Mama was crying, crying without making a sound. She held Johann close to her chest, rocking back and forth, tears rolling down her cheeks.

Nettie felt a sharp pain in her stomach. She couldn't recall ever seeing Mama cry before. Silently, Nettie took bread and cheese and *pluma moos* from the pantry and set it on the table. She put bowls and cups on the table, and boiled water in the samovar. Then she went and looked at her baby brother. He wasn't crying. He looked white, almost as white as the snow outside. His only movements were tiny breaths, so faint that Nettie wasn't sure at first that he was breathing at all.

The door to the schoolroom opened and her father came in. "Dinner's ready," whispered Nettie, her eyes on Johann.

"I'm not hungry," said Mama, so Nettie and Papa ate alone. When they were done, Papa took his son and held him till it was time to go back to school.

February 22, 1918. It's quiet in our house without Johann. I don't want Mama to have any more babies. It's too sad when they die.

CHAPTER 7

March 14, 1918. Lena's house is full of relatives. She came to our house because it is quieter. We had tea with my tea set from Aunt Nettie.

Two sets of uncles and aunts and all their children had come to stay at Lena's house. Instead of having a room to herself, Lena now shared a room with three of her cousins. Two were younger than Lena and one was older.

"How long will your aunts and uncles stay?" asked Nettie. She poured tea for Lena from her small china teapot into the tiny matching teacup. After pouring her own cup, she set the pot down and looked at Lena.

"I don't know," said Lena. "I wish they would go home today. It's too noisy. There are too many people."

"Your brothers probably don't mind," suggested Nettie.

"No," agreed Lena. "They're boys."

She chose a piece of bread and butter from the bowl Nettie offered her and set it on her plate.

When her relatives first arrived, Lena had been excited. It was good to have cousins come to visit, especially cousins from so far away.

When they stayed and stayed, Lena wasn't quite so excited.

"Why did they come?" asked Nettie.

"To visit, of course." Lena pressed her lips together firmly and looked down at her plate.

"That's all?" Nettie watched as Lena picked up the bread and started shredding it between her fingers. "Just to visit?"

"Yes," said Lena. "What other reason could there be?" She looked down at the crumbs on her tiny painted plate. Suddenly her eyes filled with tears. "Oh, Nettie, I'm so scared. I heard my father and my uncles talking in the night. Bad things are happening in some of the villages. People steal things and hurt other people, and some people were killed." She wiped her eyes with her sleeve and looked up at Nettie. "I don't want them to go if they're going to *die!*"

Nettie didn't know what to say. Finally she stood up and walked around the table. She put her arms around Lena, and was surprised to find they were both crying.

After Lena went home, Nettie went to the schoolroom to find her father. He was preparing his lessons for the next day but smiled at Nettie when she came in.

"Did you enjoy your tea party with Lena?" he asked.

Nettie barely heard him. "Why are Lena's aunts and uncles here?" she asked. "Does someone want to kill them?"

Papa didn't answer right away. He closed his books and piled them on top of each other neatly, making sure the edges were all straight. When they were perfect, he looked at Nettie. "Is that what Lena told you?" he asked.

"She said people are hurting and stealing and killing."

Papa shook his head and muttered something Nettie couldn't understand.

"Some people don't know how to behave," he began slowly. "Some people don't know how to be kind, or how to do what's right. And some people don't know how to work for what they need."

Nettie waited.

"There are —" Papa paused as if searching for a word, "bad things happening in some of our colonies. The new government appointed councils to lead the different areas of the country. Some of the men on the councils are uneducated. They don't know how to be leaders. They use their authority to help themselves and to hurt people who have more money than they do."

"They don't like rich people?" asked Nettie. "Is Lena's family rich?"

"Her uncles are landowners," said Papa. "They have beautiful houses and many horses and cows. Some of the

Ukrainian peasants used to work for the Wiebe family. That's the name of Mrs. Remple's brothers," he explained. "They were jealous that those things belonged to the Wiebes and not to the Ukrainians. And some –" he paused, and started again, "and *many* Mennonite people have not been kind to the peasants. They treated them like ani –" Papa stopped again.

"They acted as if the peasants were not people. Right now the government doesn't have control over all the country. No one is enforcing the laws. Some of the peasants have decided to get wealth for themselves by stealing. Sometimes they want to pay people back for treating them badly."

Nettie thought about what Papa said. She could see why the peasants would be angry. But even so, they shouldn't kill people. They shouldn't steal things. Papa had always told her she should pay evil with good. It seemed easier when it was just Jacob teasing her. This was too hard.

"Are there angry Ukrainian people here too, Papa?"

"There are angry people everywhere."

"But –" Nettie began and then stopped.

Her father seemed to know what she was thinking. "Pray to God," he said, "that it won't happen here."

CHAPTER 8

March 20, 1918. Ukraine is free! Every time Papa sees a news-paper there is something new. Now they tell us that several countries got their freedom from Russia when Russia pulled out of the war against Germany. They say Germany is going to send soldiers here to make sure Ukraine is safe from the Russians who might want to take it back. I would rather see no soldiers here at all, but that is never the way it is.

It was April and spring had truly arrived. Nettie noticed the apple blossoms as she met Lena outside the school one morning.

"Don't the apple trees smell wonderful?" she asked Lena.

Lena didn't take time to comment. "The German Army is here," she said.

"Where?" asked Nettie, looking around, wondering if the German Army was right in Gruenfeld. She wished that sometime she could know something before Lena did. "How do you know?"

"Papa telephoned to Moscow yesterday," said Lena. "He talked to someone there who told him all the news. He knows that Germany is helping Ukraine, now that Ukraine is no longer part of Russia."

"Everybody knows *that,*" said Nettie. "But I didn't know the Germans were here already."

"Well, they are. And they are going to make the peasants give back all the things they've stolen, so then Papa will get back his horse."

"Does he know where the horse is?"

"Oh, yes. He asked everybody who came into the mill. He found out who stole him. When the German army comes, he is going to ask them."

"Oh." Nettie didn't say so to Lena, but she thought an army was big and important. She didn't think they would care about one horse. She hoped they did, though. It wasn't right for people to take things that didn't belong to them. They even stole when people were watching and didn't care who saw. If she stole something, she would feel bad, and she knew that God would be displeased with her. Did these thieves not care about what anyone thought? Not even God?

"And maybe they will make it safe so my uncles and aunts can go home to Molotschna." The teacher appeared in the doorway then, so all the children filed into the classroom, but Nettie found herself looking around for soldiers.

Several days passed before she actually saw them.

She was working hard on her sums one morning when the class was disturbed by the sound of heavy boots in the coatroom. The door to the classroom flew open. Two men in greyish-green army uniforms stepped into the room. Nettie gasped and shrank into her seat.

The men smiled at the students and at the teacher, who looked as startled as Nettie felt. "Excuse us, Fraulein," said one of the soldiers and Nettie heard someone whisper.

"German! They're German soldiers."

Nettie had seen soldiers before, riding through the village to somewhere more important, stopping at a house to demand a drink or a meal, but none of those soldiers had spoken German. Nettie looked over at Lena. She was smiling. "See," her smile silently said to Nettie. "I was right. They are coming to get my father's horse back."

"We saw your school and thought we'd like to speak to some good German children."

I'm not German, thought Nettie. I was born in Russia. But I can't speak Russian, she added honestly. And these soldiers would not force her to learn Russian.

The soldiers talked to the students for a few minutes, telling them how much better everything would be now the Germans were in Ukraine. The boys stared in fascination at them. Have they forgotten Mennonites don't believe in fighting? wondered Nettie. The boys all looked as if they wanted to have guns and sabres and uniforms too. Nettie bent her head to her sums. She didn't look up again until the soldiers left the room. She could still hear their heavy boots, though, as they went to visit Papa's classroom next door.

April 14, 1918. Lena's cousins and aunts and uncles went home. The German army has chased the Red Bolshevik army back to Russia so it is safe for them at home again. Lena is happy to have her bedroom back. The anarchist Makhno who took over the colonies east of here is gone too. I guess the German army is a good army.

June 2, 1918. I helped weed the gardens again today. Everything is getting very tall, even the weeds. Sara, Abram, and Jacob are home from school.

Nettie could hardly wait for the day that Sara came home from school. She was glad to see Abram and Jacob too, but it was Sara she was most eager to see. Liese brought over syrup cookies and Mama had coffee waiting when they arrived home. They all sat around the table talking until it was time to make supper. Then Liese helped Mama prepare the meal while Nettie and Sara went out to the garden.

"I tried to care for your flowers," Nettie told Sara. "I pulled out lots of weeds."

"That's good," said Sara. "Did you pull out any flowers?"

"No!" exclaimed Nettie. "At least I hope not. Sometimes when they're little it's hard to tell."

"Don't worry, I was just teasing you. Some flowers make so many seeds you have to pull out some of them. Like the poppies. There are always too many poppies."

"The snowdrops are done blooming," said Nettie, "and I helped plant the vegetable garden and the watermelons."

"I see you're becoming a good helper. Do you want to show me what's growing?"

Sara seemed glad to be back with her flowers. She smiled as she knelt beside the pansies and the lilies of the valley. "There are still some tulips blooming," Nettie told her eagerly. "On the other side of the house."

The sound of horses drowned out Sara's reply. When she spoke again, her voice was cold. "Soldiers."

"They're German soldiers," explained Nettie in case Sara didn't know. "They aren't the kind that steal from people."

"Is that right?" asked Sara. She turned back to her flowers, but Nettie went to peer around the mulberry hedge. She watched as the soldiers pulled to a stop by the mill. They got off their horses and spoke to a couple of farmers delivering grain. A group of younger men joined them. Nettie could hardly see the soldiers in the centre of the group.

"Sara," she said suddenly, her eyes on one of the men. "It looks like Abram talking to the soldiers."

"Abram!" exclaimed Sara. Her head jerked up. "It can't be," she said. "Abram doesn't believe in fighting. He wouldn't stand around listening to the bragging of soldiers."

"How do you know they're bragging?"

"What else could they be doing? Here, look. These insects think they should eat my flowers."

"I'm going over there to see," said Nettie, ignoring Sara. She moved around the bushes, her eyes fixed on the man who looked like Abram. Only he couldn't be a man, because Abram wasn't a man, was he? He was just a boy, like Jacob.

"No!" said Sara, but it was too late. Nettie was already darting across the street.

"You must protect yourselves," one of the soldiers said as Nettie came up behind him. "We can't be everywhere, there aren't enough of us. Makhno's anarchists will come again. You must be prepared."

The men moved around as others joined the group. It took Nettie a moment to find him, but sure enough, there was Abram, listening intently, his eyes never leaving the soldier's face.

He looked different from last fall when he went away to school. He'd turned eighteen while he was gone, and eighteen was a man, even if it seemed impossible that her brother could be so old. At the house he'd smiled as if he was glad to be home, but now his smile was gone.

When she crossed the street, Nettie thought she was going to take Abram's hand and lead him home. Now that she was here, she knew she couldn't do it. Instead she backed away from the group, then ran, panting, back to Sara.

"So?" said Sara.

"It was Abram," said Nettie, her voice ragged. She dropped to the ground beside Sara. "He didn't know I was there."

"He's interested in many different things," said Sara. "He probably just wants to listen."

"I guess so," said Nettie.

She and Sara weeded in the soft, damp soil until Mama called them in for supper. Nettie was surprised to find Abram already in the house, talking with Papa and Peter. Everyone gathered around the table enjoying the cottage cheese-filled *vereneki* with sour cream and thick slices of fried ham. No one mentioned the soldiers.

CHAPTER 9

July 10, 1918. It was hot today and I went in Lena's pool. It is in the yard behind the mill with trees and grass all around it. I don't have a bathing costume so I had to borrow one from Lena. I felt bare in it, though it covered my arms and legs. I was glad there was no one there to watch us. Lena can swim but I just splashed.

Papa was not so busy in the summer when there was no school. When Nettie was younger, Papa and Mama had always gone for a holiday in the summer. They went south to the Black Sea where they enjoyed different weather and different people and different food. When they came home, they had grapes or oranges tucked in with their clothes. They hadn't gone south in the last couple of years, maybe because of the war, or maybe because sending their children away to school cost too much money.

Instead Papa worked in the garden, hoeing the vegetables till not one weed showed in the neat rows. They had another garden on the edge of the village, part of the community garden. They grew potatoes and watermelon there. Papa kept that garden as neat as the one at home.

In the afternoons when the sun was hot, he walked over to Mr. Neufeld's store and drank coffee with some of the men there. Other times Papa read books. If Nettie couldn't find him in the house or the garden and it wasn't coffee time, she often found him in the shade of a tree, reading a book.

He seldom went to the schoolroom in the summer. That's where Mama kept the silkworms. Big wooden trays covered the tops of the desks, holding the worms as they munched their way through the mulberry leaves. Later the worms spun cocoons. Mama and Sara dipped the cocoons into hot water to kill the larvae and soften the silk. Then they unwound the long strand of silk. That thread was too thin to sew with, so Mama spun several threads together on the spinning wheel to make sewing thread.

Usually Nettie stayed away from the worms. When she went into the schoolroom, she could hear them chewing the leaves. She didn't like hearing chewing from so many small creatures.

Sara liked the worms almost as much as she liked her flowers. When the worms were small, she fed them mulberry leaves, but when they were bigger she cut whole branches off the trees. Nettie had watched her lay a branch among the worms, then smile as they crawled over it.

Nettie peeked in at the worms one day and noticed the branches were almost bare. She found a basket and went out to the bushes behind the house to pick leaves for the silkworms.

She glanced at the garden as she carried her basket past it. Papa was leaning against the pear tree, his hoe clutched in his left hand. Nettie thought she knew why. The rows of cabbages and sorrel and dill and beans looked perfect already. He must be waiting for another weed to grow so he could immediately hoe it up. Giggling at her own thought, Nettie called, "Hi, Papa," and stepped between two mulberry bushes to begin gathering leaves.

"Strange," she thought. "that silkworms only eat mulberry leaves." She held one up and looked at it before taking a tiny nibble out of the corner. "Phooey. *Borscht* tastes much better," she said, thinking of the soup they'd had for dinner, "And so does applesauce, and fried ham, and *pluma moos."* With each leaf she picked, she thought of another food she liked better. The more leaves she picked, the more she wondered about worms that only liked one food when she liked so many.

"Ammonia cookies," she said out loud, thinking of the big white peppermint-flavoured cookies her mother always made at Christmas time, "and *plautz,"* she added, wishing she had a piece of the sweet, fruit-covered bread right now.

When her basket was half full, Nettie decided she'd picked enough leaves for the worms. She walked around the end of the hedge and was surprised to see that Papa was sprawled on the ground under the tree.

"Papa," she cried, suddenly alarmed. "Are you all right? Is something wrong?"

Papa slowly looked up and shook his head at Nettie. "No," he said, his voice very slow. "I'm just thinking."

He pushed his left hand into the ground, trying to stand up, but he couldn't seem to move.

"Papa!" Nettie cried again. "What can I do?"

"Just – just give me your hand," he said, his voice, weak and uneven. "I-I must be tired."

He stretched his left hand out to Nettie. She took it. Working together and with much heavy breathing, Papa got to his feet.

Papa asked Nettie for the hoe. He took it in his left hand, leaning heavily on it for a moment. Finally he took a step forward, still leaning on the hoe. Nettie reached out to hold his other hand, his right hand. She squeezed his fingers but his hand stayed limp in hers. Slowly they moved across the yard.

Papa left the hoe by the door, but held onto the door frame as he went into the house.

Nettie watched as the door closed behind her father, then went back for the basket of leaves. Neither Sara nor

Mama was anywhere in sight, so Nettie went into the schoolroom on her own. She walked around, placing the leaves wherever she saw worms. They were soon munching away on the new leaves, leaving the old, wrinkly ones still on the branches.

Papa didn't come to the table at suppertime. Mama brought a plate to him in the bedroom. "Is Papa sick?" asked Sara when Mama came back. Mama shook her head. "No," she said quickly. "He's just tired."

But Nettie remembered the slow way Papa had walked across the yard and the strange way his hand had felt in hers. She was sure something was wrong.

Sara hadn't seen Papa lying under the pear tree, so she didn't know what was wrong. She put down her cup of tea and smiled at Mama. "Something odd happened in the schoolroom today," she said. "Someone fed the worms. There were individual leaves scattered all over the trays."

"I wouldn't do so much work," said Mama. "If I cut the branch, the worms can pick their own leaves."

"I agree," said Sara. She smiled at Nettie. "I can't think who would have picked the leaves for the worms."

Nettie sat quietly in her chair and didn't say a word.

CHAPTER 10

July 15, 1918. I've hardly seen Papa all week. Today he came out to the front room. Mama says he is better, but he still walks so slow. He doesn't work and he doesn't smile.

The last thing Papa did each night before he went to bed was wind the Kroeger clock. Nettie loved the clock, with its long pendulum, four hanging weights, and roses painted on its face. It hung in the front room, faithfully ticking, a background to everything the family did. Every sixty minutes, the deep bonging marked the hour.

While Papa rested in his bed, Mama asked Abram to wind the clock. Abram wound it five times before Papa did it himself again.

The whole family walked to church together Sunday morning. Mama, Nettie, Sara, and Liese all sat together on one of the hard benches. Jacob thought he was a man now that he went away to school, so he sat with the other men.

Nettie listened carefully as the minister described what the Bible said about fighting. "Love your enemies," he said, "and do good to those who persecute you." Nettie thought of the soldiers in the street and wondered what Abram was thinking.

August 23, 1918. I thought the war was over, but Mennonite boys are marching with the German soldiers.

Nettie tried not to think about the war, but there was always something to remind her. One evening she saw soldiers marching in the street. Some older boys were marching with them. Later that evening Papa called Abram into the front room.

"We don't have guns, Papa."

Mama sewed while Nettie made new clothes for her paper dolls. They both pretended they couldn't hear what was going on in the other room.

"It doesn't matter," said Papa. His voice was firmer and stronger than Nettie had heard it in weeks. "You are marching with soldiers. You are talking to soldiers. Pretty soon you will be thinking like the soldiers."

"Maybe that's a good thing." Abram spoke urgently and Nettie noticed how alike he and Papa sounded. "Do you think Russia is going to sit back and let Ukraine be independent? Of course not, they need the food we grow here. The German army won't be here long. They are losing the war with the rest of Europe. The Bolshevik soldiers are going to come back here – to Gruenfeld – and we must be prepared. Makhno and men like him will come back. We must be prepared. When the Germans leave, the only ones who can help us will be ourselves."

"But Abram." Her father's voice was quiet. Nettie strained her ears to hear. "We believe that when someone takes your cloak, offer him your robe too. When someone strikes one cheek, turn your face so he can also strike the other one."

"Yes," said Abram. "And when thieves walk in here with their sabres and their pistols, are you going to turn the other cheek as they reach for Mama and Sara and Nettie?"

"Hey, why's it so quiet in here?" With a loud stamping of his feet and a slamming of the door, Jacob stepped into the house. "Where's Abram? I need to tell him about Isaac's foal. It's only five months old and already it –" Jacob stopped and looked at his mother and sisters. "Is something wrong? Is Papa –"

"Your papa is fine," said Mama. "He's talking to Abram in the other room. Do you want something to eat?"

"Oh sure, Mama. Nothing much, I had *faspa* at the farm. Maybe just some bread and ham and *moos*. Oh, and if there's some of that plum *plautz* left, that would sure be good. No one makes plum *plautz* like you." He dug out a fork and a spoon and reached for a plate. "So what is Papa telling Abram? It won't do any good, you know. Abram gets his own ideas and nothing changes him."

Mama cut thick slices from the round, flat loaf of rye bread and spread them with butter. "What your papa says to your brother is not your business," said Mama. She smiled at Jacob to soften her words. "Just like it's not his business what Papa says to you."

"Yes, but Papa only says one thing to me. 'No, Jacob,'" he mimicked his father's voice, "'we do not need a horse. We cannot afford a horse. You must marry a rich man's daughter and then you can buy a horse.'"

Nettie broke out laughing at the last sentence and even Mama had a twinkle in her eye as she reprimanded Jacob. "Your father never told you to marry a rich man's daughter, don't tell lies."

"No, Mama," said Jacob in mock contrition, "I won't tell lies." He took a big bite of bread. "But someday I will have horses." He winked at Nettie, "and maybe I will marry a rich man's daughter."

"There is no need to talk of marrying, my little rooster. You are only fourteen."

"But such a big healthy boy, eh, Mama?" laughed Jacob, and Mama gave him a little slap on the side of his head that just made him laugh more.

It was hard to remember Jacob was only fourteen – he was as big as Abram already. Nettie guessed he took after Mama's side of the family, as neither Papa nor Abram were big men. Papa never seemed short, though. He walked very straight, and to Nettie he always looked distinguished, with his neat clothes and his small, pointed beard.

Laughing with Jacob made Nettie forget Abram and the frightening things he said, but as Jacob ate, the sinking feeling in her stomach returned. How could Abram think like a soldier? He was a scholar, a student. He wanted to go to the university. And besides, thought Nettie, remembering what was surely the most important thing of all, Mennonites did not believe in fighting or killing. Mennonites could not be soldiers.

All summer, Abram spent his free time with his friends from school and the German soldiers.

Papa said less and less, not just to Abram but to everyone. One day when Nettie came up behind Papa as he sat at his big desk in the front room, she saw that he was writing on a slate. Nettie glanced at the slate. Papa's letters looked worse than Nettie's had when she first learned to write. They were big and sprawling and didn't stay in neat lines. Then Nettie saw he was writing with his left hand, while his right arm hung limp at his side.

"That looks like hard work, Papa." Nettie took a slate and chalk and tried writing with her left hand. It was even harder than she'd thought it would be. She made an *A* and a *B* and looked at Papa's. Compared to hers, his didn't look so bad anymore.

"The letters want to go backwards," she complained. "And they won't stay beside each other."

Papa nodded. "I know," he said. "My letters won't go where I want them either."

He wrote his name, and Nettie's name, and then the names of all the members of the family. He erased them and wrote the alphabet and a Bible verse. Nettie could see it was hard for Papa. She wanted to ask why he was doing it, but when she looked at his limp right arm, she knew that Papa was not just writing with his left hand because he liked to try new things.

When her left hand grew tired from the unusual work, Nettie went outside. She found Sara hoeing around the vegetables. "The weeds are gone in the flower beds," she said, "but I saw some here." For a moment Nettie was surprised that Sara could find a weed in Papa's vegetable garden. Then she realized that hoeing would be difficult with one arm. She crouched down and pulled small weeds from among the cabbage plants. It felt good to help Papa, even when he didn't know.

CHAPTER 11

September 3, 1918. Jacob and Sara went away to school but Abram stayed home. He is finished at the business school. Maybe he can go to university next year. For that he might go to Europe.

"You're old enough to be my helper now," said Papa. "It will be your job to clean in the classroom. You must sweep the floor and erase the chalkboard each day."

Nettie stared at Papa in surprise. What about the Ukrainian girl who always came to clean each day after school?

Papa smiled. "Why do we need someone else when we have a girl right here who can do just as good a job?"

Nettie liked to help Papa. He asked her to erase the chalkboard first. While she was sweeping the floor, he painstakingly wrote the next day's assignments on the board with his left hand. He couldn't hold a book in his right hand, so he put it on a chair nearby where he could consult it as he wrote. The letters Papa put on the board were neater than the ones he had been practising that day at his desk at home.

Nettie looked at them and thought proudly that no one would guess he had written them with his left hand.

When the classroom was clean, they walked home together, out the door, down the path, then in the front door.

"Why didn't we go through the connecting door?" Nettie asked as Papa reached his hand towards the building for support.

"I need to move more," said Papa. His eyes twinkled. "If I don't walk, my old bones might forget how."

"Oh," said Nettie. She opened the door and let Papa go in first. He moved more slowly than he used to, but stood just as straight. Nettie could see how hard he worked to make his right leg move the way it should.

Each day after that, Nettie cleaned the classroom. When Papa was finished writing on the board, he listened to Nettie's lessons. She had already recited them to her teacher, but Papa had her say them again. He wanted to be sure she was learning properly. Nettie recited all her lessons, pleased when Papa was pleased, and determined to do better when he frowned. She often had trouble with the Russian words, but Papa helped her till she said them perfectly.

Sometimes they sat for awhile on the bench outside

the door. They watched the stork on the roof of the mill and listened for the sound of the cows coming back from the pasture. After Nettie brought Blossom and Daisy into the barn, it would be time to help Mama make supper.

September 28, 1918. I see German soldiers almost every day, marching in the street or just passing through the village. Little boys see them too, then they find sticks and pretend they are guns. They put them over their shoulders and march like the soldiers. What has happened to the Mennonites who did not believe in fighting?

Nettie leaned against the wall of the school and watched the soldiers march. They didn't stay in Gruenfeld, but two or three times a week a group of them would ride into town and march in the street. Recruiting, Nettie said to herself. It was a word she'd heard her father use. She knew it meant they were looking for people to join them.

An officer stood to one side shouting orders as the soldiers marched with their backs straight, never looking to either side. She wasn't the only person watching. Two boys riding by on their bicycles stopped. Men coming from the mill looked back over their shoulders as they walked away.

On the other side of the street, several young men gathered around a wagon. Nettie knew them from church. They'd been there with the soldiers before.

Often they joined in the marching, though they didn't have rifles. Today they seemed more interested in whatever was in the wagon than in the marching soldiers.

Nettie wanted to see what was in the wagon. Hiding behind bushes as much as she could, she ran down the street past several houses, then quickly darted across to the other side. There she again ducked behind bushes and wagons as she crept up on the group of men.

Nettie wasn't surprised to find Abram standing by the wagon. She was surprised, though, to see a rifle in his hands. She slipped up behind him and grabbed his arm.

"Put it down," she whispered fiercely. "You mustn't join the soldiers."

"Go home!" Abram whispered back. "You don't understand."

"Have you forgotten what Papa and the elders taught us?" asked Nettie, still tugging at the arm that held the rifle. "You mustn't fight. I don't want you to be hurt." Nettie felt tears on her cheeks and brushed them away angrily. "Leave it and come home."

Abram glanced quickly around, but the others were all watching the German soldier handing out the rifles. No one noticed them. He knelt down beside Nettie and looked into her face. "I have to stay here. I don't care if I get hurt, but I have to protect you and Mama and Papa and the others. We can't let those Makhnovites come in here like they have in so many villages."

"But Abram," Nettie began.

Abram stood up and gave her a little push. "Go home now, you're too young to understand." He turned away, then turned back quickly, "And Nettie? Don't tell Mama and Papa, it will only make them sad."

"They might see you themselves."

Abram shrugged. "I can't help that. Now go play in the sand. Don't worry about adult things."

Eyes stinging and her breathing ragged, Nettie turned around and, skirting the still-marching soldiers, went back to her house. Did he think she was still a baby, she wondered, telling her to go play in the sand? Instead, she went inside and added a note to her diary.

Abram has a German rifle. How can he be a Mennonite when he has a gun?

CHAPTER 12

November 25, 1918. The Germans are gone. If Abram is right, the Russians will send their army back into Ukraine. And what about the robbers and thieves? If there is no one here keeping order, who will protect us from the robbers and thieves?

Wherever people gathered, Nettie heard of the shock they felt when the Germans left. What would happen now?

Nettie remembered that when Abram first joined the Self-Defence Unit, he'd told Papa the Germans would not stay forever. But to leave so soon! They'd come in April, bringing peace back to the Mennonite villages, forcing Ukrainian peasants to give back livestock, farm machinery, and other things they'd stolen from the Mennonites. It didn't seem right for them to leave already.

It was not only Nettie who wondered what would happen now.

Abram had helped with harvest at Doerksens', but when the crop was in, there was no more work for him. He found a day or two of work here and there, but it wasn't much.

"I don't know why I can't find steady work," Abram said at breakfast one morning. "The Ukrainians won't work for German-speaking people anymore. There should be work for all us landless Mennonites."

Nettie looked up from her fried potatoes. Abram sounded bitter.

"You'll find work," Mama said comfortingly. "You're a good worker. Someone will need you. Have you asked Herman Remple at the mill?"

"He keeps his men forever," said Abram. His teeth flashed briefly in something that was almost a smile. "He'll only need me when one of the old men can't lift a bag of flour anymore. Or maybe he will use smaller bags so they can still carry them."

December 1, 1918. Teacher gave us our Christmas Wishes to learn. Mine is much longer than last year's. She didn't have the beautiful folders we usually cover them with, but we will still copy them in our best writing so Mama and Papa will remember what we said.

The Wishes were special poems children learned at Christmas time. They recited them on Christmas Day, first for their parents, then for any friends or relatives who asked to hear them. Nettie and Lena practised their verses by saying them to each other. When Nettie had hers almost perfect, she recited it for Liese.

"You recite beautifully," Liese told her when she finished.

"I've said it a hundred times at least," replied Nettie. "Lena and I say our poems to each other at recess and at lunchtime."

"That's the best way to learn." Liese smiled. "Mama and Papa will be very proud of you. I know I am."

"You need a baby to say a Wish for you," said Nettie.

Liese's cheeks turned pink, but she laughed. "Silly, babies can't talk."

"No, but they grow big and then they give their mamas Wishes for Christmas."

"Maybe someday," said Liese. She stood up and went to the cupboard. "But now, would you like a cookie? I made ammonia cookies this morning and they taste just like Mama's."

The day before Sara and Jacob came home, Nettie found herself extra busy after school. She helped Papa in the schoolroom as they got ready for the Christmas program. By the time she'd recited her lessons to Papa and reviewed her Wish by herself, she was late helping Mama make supper. She rushed into the kitchen to find Mama taking bread out of the big oven. There was a bag of flour on the table and four more sitting by the door.

"That's five bags of flour, Mama," said Nettie. "Are we going to make so many Christmas cookies?"

"I'm not sure," Mama replied. "It depends on the sugar."

"On the sugar?" asked Nettie. "Don't we have any? Can't we buy some more? We can make syrup cookies, we still have lots of watermelon syrup."

"I'll have to see," said Mama. She glanced at the bags of flour. "Maybe we can buy some sugar. I'd like to make ammonia cookies."

Nettie patted the top of one of the flour bags. "Why are these here, Mama?" she asked. "Shouldn't they be in the attic?" And why so many? Nettie wondered to herself. Usually the Pauls family had just two sacks of flour at a time, rye flour for bread and wheat flour for all the other baking. When a sack was empty, Papa went to the mill for another.

"Yes," Mama said slowly. "Abram can do it when he comes home. Perhaps we'll keep a sack or two down here. We may take some to trade for sugar and other things."

"Like you do when we have too much butter?" asked Nettie. She knew how that worked. When both their cows were milking at the same time, Mama would make far more butter than the family could eat. She took the extra butter to the market. Someone without a cow might buy it, or someone whose cow was going to have a new calf and couldn't be milked.

"Yes, that's right," said Mama. "This time when the school board paid Papa, they paid him in flour. We'll see if we can trade our flour for groceries, just like we do sometimes with butter and eggs."

As Nettie peeled potatoes, she wondered about being paid with flour. Surely it was easier to pay with rubles. They took up much less space and were easier to carry around.

CHAPTER 13

January 16, 1919. Sara and Jacob didn't go back to school. Papa said it's not a good time to travel. I know it's winter, but they travelled in winter before. There must be another reason.

"Is it really a bad time to travel?" asked Nettie. She looked at the plate she was washing to make sure it was clean. Jacob sat by the table working on his harness. The harness would be finished one day, but Nettie couldn't see any sign of a horse, especially if Papa was being paid in flour. How much flour did it take to buy a horse?

Jacob grunted.

"It's winter," said Nettie. "And it's cold." She dried the plate and set it on top of the last one. "But it was winter and cold when you came home before Christmas, and winter when you went to school last year. That can't be why."

Jacob let the harness drop to the floor and leaned back in his chair. "It's the Makhnovites," he said. "Papa doesn't want us to travel because of the bandits. They stop wagons on the road, they steal the horses, they take people's coats and boots and food, and they leave them there. Sometimes they kill people. That's why Papa didn't want us to go to school."

"Oh." Nettie thought for a moment. "I thought the Volunteer Army kept the roads safe."

"We'd like that," said Jacob. He held the piece of harness up and looked critically at it. "Unfortunately, the bandits are sometimes stronger than Denikin's Army."

"That's good then."

"Good there are dangerous bandits?" Jacob looked surprised. "What kind of child are you?"

Nettie flicked her towel at Jacob. "Foolish boy," she said, trying to sound like her mother. "I meant it's good you didn't go to school."

As she dried the rest of the dishes, Nettie wondered if the bandits were the only reason Papa hadn't let Jacob and Sara go to school. She remembered the bags of flour. They had traded one bag and bought sugar and other things for Christmas. Mama had bought cloth and made Nettie and Sara and Liese new aprons, as well as handkerchiefs for Jacob and Abram, Peter, and Papa. But could someone pay for Central School with flour? Probably not, she decided.

Footsteps behind her caused Nettie to turn around. Abram, dressed in his high boots, fur hat, and warm overcoat, reached for the door latch.

"Going somewhere?" asked Jacob. "Can I come?"

"Not tonight," said Abram. "I'll be gone till after midnight."

"Oh?"

"We've decided to patrol the villages," Abram explained briefly. He glanced at Nettie and lowered his voice slightly. "Makhnovites have been seen in the area."

Jacob nodded. He, too, glanced at Nettie. She knew they'd say more if she wasn't there, but she wanted to know what was going on. "I've heard about the Molotschna," Jacob said.

"It's not just there. Chortitza, too."

Chortitza. That was where Sara's school was. What a good thing Papa hadn't let Sara go back.

"Are there many of them here?" Nettie asked urgently. "How can you stop them?" Nettie knew Abram didn't have a rifle in the house, but did he store it somewhere else?

"We'll stop them," said Abram firmly. He looked at Nettie for a moment, then added, "They probably won't stay around here. Gruenfeld is a small village. What would they want with such a place?" Before Nettie could answer, he was out the door and gone.

February 12, 1919. Abram goes out every night to patrol the village. He carries the German rifle. He has not shot anyone. He has not even seen a Makhnovite.

As long as Nettie could remember, a Ukrainian washerwoman had done their laundry. Every six weeks she came to their house to wash all the dirty clothes and linens. Today, however, Mama said they didn't need her. Why should they pay for someone to do work they could do themselves?

"With you girls to help, it will be easy," she said. Sara and Nettie looked at each other silently. Sara's face didn't show her feelings, but Nettie was sure she felt the same inside as Nettie did. What a terrible job. And in winter, too.

The laundry soaked in big tubs full of water and the soap Mama made from melted fat and wood ashes. Nettie and Sara rubbed the clothes on the washboards till Mama said they were clean. Then they went into the rinse water. Though he protested, even Jacob helped. He carried in the pails of water that Mama heated on the stove. When he wasn't carrying water, he was bringing in more fuel for the fire. The fuel was made in the summer by mixing straw with the manure from the cows. When it was dry, it was cut in squares and stacked for burning through the winter. On laundry day the fire burned constantly to heat the big kettles full of water.

When Mama decided the clothes were rinsed enough, they were wrung out by hand. Nettie tried to twist the water out of the clothes but Mama said her hands were too small. Mama and Sara twisted and squeezed till not another drop would come out. Then Sara and Nettie lugged the baskets of wet clothing out into the cold yard.

There wasn't room for all the laundry on the clothesline. The sheets were draped over bushes or laid on the snow.

They froze almost instantly into stiff boards.

"I'm glad we don't have to sleep on these tonight," said Nettie as she rushed back to the house. "They won't dry until spring."

While Mama and Jacob emptied the wash water, Sara and Nettie put clean sheets on the feather mattresses, and fluffed the pillows and quilts.

Abram and Jacob's bed in the barn had the most quilts of all. They always slept in the barn in the summer, but this year Mama had said they must continue even when it was cold. "We don't want anyone to steal our cows," she said. Nettie's brothers didn't protest. They just did what Mama said. Nettie thought of men with guns and prayed every day for safety for Abram and Jacob as they slept in the loft.

Now she realized she must also pray for them to stay warm. "How can they sleep out here?" she demanded, as she and Sara spread the last quilt. "They will die of the cold."

"They sleep in their clothes," said Sara.

Nettie was shocked. "How do you know?"

Sara smiled. "Didn't you notice how dirty their sheets were when we took them off?"

Nettie nodded thoughtfully. Sleeping in their clothes made sense. Not only would they be warmer while they slept, but they wouldn't have the shock of cold when they dressed. Nettie wondered if she could sleep in her clothes too.

Glancing at Sara, she decided not. Sara wouldn't approve.

Nettie's first thought on waking the next morning was relief that it was not washday again. She went to school while Mama and Sara took turns pressing the clean clothes with an iron heated on the stove. The sheets and tablecloths were spread around the house to finish drying, then Mama and Sara carried them to Friesens', where they were put through the mangle to make them smooth.

It was Saturday morning when Abram didn't come for breakfast.

"Where is Abram?" Mama asked briskly. She put a plate of fried potatoes in front of Jacob and told Nettie to sit up straighter. Nettie straightened her back and tried not to yawn. "I thought he was working at the mill today," Mama went on.

"No," said Jacob. He glanced at Papa, but Papa was intent on lifting his fork with his right hand and didn't seem to be paying attention. "Mr. Remple told him last night he wouldn't need him after all," Jacob said. "Abram left early this morning."

"Left?" Mama put the pot on the stove and dropped into her chair. "What do you mean left? He went looking for work? He went for a walk?"

"He didn't say," said Jacob. Nettie saw him glance sideways at Papa again. "I woke up early this morning. He had the bag he used to take his clothes to school. I asked him what he was doing. He was surprised I was awake. He said he had to go away, but not to worry and he would write. I asked him where he was going, but he didn't answer."

The water in the samovar was boiling, but Mama didn't notice. Nettie slipped out of her seat and made the tea.

"Did you hear that, Abram?" Mama asked. "Did you hear what Jacob said?"

"I heard," said Papa heavily.

"He may be looking for work," said Nettie out loud. Inside she thought, "He may join the army." Even though he was a Mennonite, he had practised with the German army, and when the Germans left, he'd joined the Self-Defence Unit. Though stories came about terrors in other villages, there had been none in Gruenfeld. Instead of waiting for evil to come to Gruenfeld, had he gone to fight it elsewhere? Nettie didn't know if she should be angry at Abram, or proud of him.

CHAPTER 14

March 5, 1919. There are armies everywhere. The Ukrainian Independence Army is trying to keep Ukraine free. The Bolshevik Red Army is trying to turn everyone into Communists. The Volunteer Army, that's the Whites, I think they want to bring back the czar, only it will have to be a new czar because the old one is dead. And of course there is Makhno's Army, though they are more like murderers and thieves. People say all the armies kill people who get in their way and steal anything they want. When soldiers come into town, I always hide.

Nettie prayed for Abram's safety every day but she didn't talk about him; neither did anyone else. Knowing about the battles going on around them added an unnatural feel to the days. Life went on as usual, but always there was the fear that something terrible could happen any moment. Nettie and Papa went to school. Jacob visited friends or tried to find work. Sara helped

Mama around the house or visited with Liese. Liese was expecting a baby and was often tired, so she appreciated Sara's help.

Two evenings a week Sara put on her winter coat and hat and, taking her muff, went to choir practice. Almost every evening Nettie worked on a tiny quilt she was making for Liese's new baby. It was made from squares of cloth saved from dresses that were too small or too worn. When she tired of sewing, she read the newspaper out loud. Mama listened while she sewed. Papa sat on the bench by the big stove and stared at the floor. Nettie thought he listened too.

Often Jacob came home with stories of bandits and people being hurt or even murdered, but as soon as he started speaking Mama would tell him to be quiet. "We cannot help it; we need not discuss it," she said. So Sara and Nettie talked with Jacob quietly when Mama and Papa were not around. Nettie thought of her aunts and uncles, grandparents and cousins, and wondered how they were. And she thought of Abram.

About a month after Abram left, they received a letter from him. He said he was well and doing what he believed was right. Nettie and Jacob, talking while feeding and milking the cows, decided this meant he had joined the army. They could only assume it was the Volunteers, the White Army that was fighting against the Bolsheviks. Jacob said that Abram had not written more in case the Bolsheviks read the letter. Nettie could not imagine anyone reading other people's letters, but Jacob probably knew what he was talking about.

Spring came, the snow melted, and the leaves came out on the trees. Nettie didn't have to worry about Jacob freezing in the barn, and Papa seemed to move around more easily.

Each day after school he sat outside on the bench by the door until Mama called him in for supper. He liked to watch the birds and often called Nettie over to see something special.

They were watching a skylark in the pear tree one afternoon when they heard horses in the street. There was shouting and the sound of a cracking whip. Nettie felt her stomach clench and stared at Papa.

"Go into the house," said Papa. He stood and moved slowly towards the door. Nettie started to follow him, then stopped. She had to see what was happening. She darted away and around the school to a spot where she could see through the newly leafed mulberry bushes.

There were several horses and riders in the street, milling around as the men talked. Behind them she could see a troika loaded with more men. Some looked like soldiers, but they weren't wearing matching uniforms. Others dressed in brightly coloured shirts, wide pants, and wide red belts. Each man had a rifle and a sword. Some waved pistols in the air. One of the men carried a black flag.

Nettie could hear their loud voices but not what they were saying. As she watched, three men broke away from the group and headed towards the mill. With relief Nettie saw that they were not going to the part where Lena and her family lived, but to the storehouse where Mr. Remple kept the flour.

Loud voices yelled inside the mill, but before anyone came out, Nettie heard a low voice behind her. "Nettie, come into the house," said Sara. "You mustn't be outside when those ruffians are here." Sara was standing by the school, out of sight of the men on the road and obviously reluctant to take another step.

Nettie glanced back at the street. The men who had not gone to the mill broke into groups of twos or threes and headed towards different houses. None looked their way. The men in the mill were still yelling. Nettie backed away from the bushes, her eyes on the street. As she joined Sara by the school, a wagon came out of the mill pulled by two horses. The wagon was heaped high with sacks of flour and one of the uniformed men was riding on each side.

The men laughed and spoke loudly but Nettie understood only a few words. Not German, not Russian; they were speaking the Ukrainian of the local peasants.

With Sara's hand gripping her arm, the two girls ran around the school and back into the house. Mama met them at the door. "Into the schoolroom," she told them. "Get down behind Papa's desk."

"But Mama," asked Nettie. "What about you and Papa?"

"Your father is lying down. I will open the door for them," said Mama. She looked fierce, but Nettie knew the look was for the thieves and robbers on the street, not for her and Sara. "Quickly! Go!" She pulled the door of the schoolroom behind her and Nettie heard her firm footsteps fading away as she and Sara squatted down behind the desk.

It was an agony, waiting in the dim schoolroom, hearing sounds outside but not knowing what was happening. Nettie imagined the men banging on the door, Mama opening it, the men coming in. Then what? She hadn't heard any shots, the men she'd seen hadn't seemed angry. Maybe they were just having a good time. Maybe they wouldn't steal anything. Maybe –

There was a loud banging on the door of the house. Louder than Nettie expected. She peered around the corner of the desk. A strip of light showed at the door. It was not closed properly. She could hear the voices of the men at the door. They were speaking Russian now, not Ukrainian. Mama didn't know much Russian. Nettie wondered how she would understand them.

"We need to eat," came a loud voice. "What do you have for us?"

"I have soup," Mama replied in Low German. *"Borscht.* And bread."

"Now, that sounds good after a cold ride," said another man, switching to *Plautdietsch* himself. Maybe he had worked for German-speaking people. "What do you say, Mitka? Shall we have some soup?"

"Is it hot?"

"Yes," said Mama. "It's very hot."

Nettie heard the men come in, their boots clumping loudly across the floor, then she heard the scrape of the chairs. After that there was a long time when the only sounds were the tinkling of spoons against bowls and grunts of pleasure.

"They're eating our soup," Nettie whispered indignantly to Sara. "What are we going to have for supper?"

"Be glad if you are alive to eat supper," Sara whispered back. "Now be quiet till they leave."

Nettie listened to the small sounds while her legs became numb. She moved around till she could sit flat, her legs out in front of her. "Sit still," Sara hissed in her ear.

"I can't," said Nettie. "My legs hurt."

"They'll hurt worse —" said Sara, but then she stopped. "Okay, but when we hear the men moving again, you must make yourself as small as you can under the desk."

Nettie nodded, feeling hungrier every moment. She thought she could smell the soup all the way into the schoolroom, and her stomach rumbled in hunger. She clutched it tightly with her arms, trying to stop the noise. What if the bandits did come in here, what would they do?

There was a loud scraping of a chair and then the sound of a man in boots moving around. "Where is the man of the house?" he asked, and Nettie jumped, for the voice sounded loud in the silent room.

"He's not well," said Mama. "He is resting."

"I must meet this man who leaves his wife to greet the guests," said the same voice. Nettie heard the other men laugh and shove their chairs back as well. Remembering Sara's words, she pulled herself up into as tiny a space as she could and listened, her heart beating so loudly in her ears that she wondered why it didn't block the sounds.

"No!" said Nettie's mother.

"No?" said the man. "Are you saying *no* to me?"

"Yes." Nettie was proud to hear her mother's voice sound so firm. "He's not well," she said again. "You've had your soup, please go."

"Who do you think you are?" asked one of the other men. "We are friends of Makhno. We do what we want. We don't listen to little German women."

"Or big German women either," said one of the others, and all the men laughed. Nettie wondered about Papa. It was not like Papa to stay hidden while these men talked rudely to Mama.

"Let's find her man," shouted one of the men. Nettie heard heavy footsteps as apparently all the men started walking forward.

"No!" said Mama. "If you want my husband, you will have to kill me first."

Nettie felt like a fist had punched her in the stomach. What was Mama saying? These men would kill her without a second thought. She had heard enough stories from Jacob to know that killing meant nothing to Makhno's men.

Instead of the sound of gunshot, Nettie heard a man's loud laughter. "This is a brave woman," a man exclaimed, adding more in Ukrainian that Nettie didn't understand. Nettie imagined Mama standing in the doorway, filling the doorway, keeping the men from going into the room where they would find Papa. The men would be standing around her with their guns and their swords, deciding what to do.

"Okay, okay, you made us good soup and we're feeling friendly. We'll leave you and your husband alone today. But another day, don't be so sure. Another day we might not be so peaceful."

There was more loud laughter and heavy footsteps, then the slam of the door. The men were gone.

Nettie stood up but Sara pulled her down. "Wait," she said. "Just because those men are gone doesn't mean there won't be more." Nettie settled back down, her head leaning against Sara, as the room slowly grew completely dark.

"COME, LITTLE ONES. It's safe to come out." With a start Nettie sat up straight, blinking in the light from the lamp Mama carried.

"Good," said Sara. "Nettie may be small but she gains weight as she sleeps."

"Are the men gone?" asked Nettie. "I didn't hear their horses."

"Yes, they're gone. You were asleep and didn't hear them." Mama straightened Nettie's skirt and patted her shoulder. "Come talk to your Papa. He's not feeling well."

Papa was lying on his bed, his face pale. He turned his head slowly as the girls came in. "Sara, Nettie. You're safe." He smiled but Nettie saw that his eyes were sad. She crawled up on the bed beside him and stroked his head.

"I'm glad you're safe too, Papa," she said. "Mama took care of all of us."

Papa stretched out his left hand to his wife. "You have the best mother and I have the best wife," he said. "Thank God." His voice faded away and his eyes closed, but the faint smile was still on his face.

CHAPTER 15

April 3, 1919. Makhno's men were here yesterday. They took flour from the mill and clothes from Schroeders and money from Friesens but only soup from us. Papa is not well but he still taught school. He moves very slowly. Jacob missed everything. He is working for Mr. Toews again. They were working with the horses and did not see the bandits.

Nettie didn't know if life could ever be the same again. It was one thing to hear of other people having troubles, but when strangers came right into her own home, threatening, and eating their food, it couldn't be forgotten so easily.

The next time Nettie saw soldiers in Gruenfeld she was visiting with Lena. The girls had set up a small table in the front room with teacups and small plates. Mrs. Remple understood that sometimes the girls needed to play where the little boys couldn't go.

Lena and Nettie pretended to be their own mothers as they fed the peppernuts and milk to Lena's rag dolls.

"And how is your garden, Mrs. Pauls?" asked Lena in her most grown-up voice.

"Very good, thank you," replied Nettie. "Everything is coming up well, and the tulips have never looked better." She took a minuscule bite of the cookie while she thought of something else to say.

"And how is business at your mill?" she said at last.

"Actually," said Lena in a low voice. "Things are not good. The government says we must share the mill with the peasants. How can we share a mill?" She was so indignant she forgot to put on her lady's voice. "You know about the robbers taking a wagonload of flour from the mill here?" Nettie nodded.

"Well, this week," Lena went on, "when Isaak Woelk took a load of flour to Chortitza, he was attacked by robbers on the road. They took the flour and the wagon and the horses too, so now we have lost two teams and wagons."

Nettie forgot her act completely. "That's horrible!" she exclaimed. "Did they hurt Mr. Woelk?"

"They cut his arm," said Lena. "But he tied it up with his handkerchief. It took him till today to get back here and he had huge sores on his feet from walking so far in his thin boots."

"But why didn't he ask for a ride?"

"He says he did," Lena said. "But people are afraid to travel far. They are afraid of the robbers." She lowered her voice. "And I think he hid when he heard horses because he thought it might be more robbers."

Nettie nodded. She would hide too. She knew she would.

The sound of horses and shouting outside interrupted their talk. Nettie felt her stomach sink with fear as she ran with Lena to the window. The street was full of men and horses.

Soldiers.

"What kind of soldiers?" whispered Nettie.

"They must be the Bolshevik soldiers," Lena whispered back, as if the uniformed men outside on their prancing horses could hear them. "They're trying to make Ukraine part of their new Russia, but Ukraine says 'no,' so they have to fight. Papa said there were some coming this way."

This was one of the groups that Abram would fight against, thought Nettie. She looked at the rifles the men carried and thought about them shooting and killing Abram. She closed her eyes, not wanting to see any more, but listening without seeing was worse. She opened her eyes again.

Some of the soldiers dismounted and left the group, walking up to houses and banging on doors. As two of them came towards Lena's house, the girls slipped down lower on the sofa so that just their eyes and the tops of their heads peeked over the back. Nettie kept her eyes on her own house across the street, but she didn't see any soldiers enter the schoolyard. She watched it so closely that when the banging came on Lena's door, she squealed in surprise.

Lena grabbed Nettie's shoulders and clung to her. "They're coming here," she whispered, her voice terrified. "Why are the soldiers coming here?"

The men banged again.

"Yes, yes, I'm coming," said Mrs. Remple in the next room. The girls heard the sound of the door opening.

"Good evening, Madam," said a soldier speaking in Russian. Nettie's Russian was not very good, but she knew the men were asking for a place to stay for a few days.

"We have no extra beds," said Mrs. Remple, sounding doubtful. Nettie and Lena looked at each other. Soldiers staying in Lena's house? Would they bring their guns into the house? It was too dreadful to contemplate.

Suddenly the door to the room burst open and both girls shrank back against the sofa. Nettie breathed more calmly when she saw that it was Mrs. Remple who had come in with such unusual force.

"Nettie," she said quickly, "you must go home; some of the soldiers are going to stay here. They are putting their horses in the barn now. Lena, come to the kitchen. I want you to stay out of sight of the soldiers. They will use your room. I'll get some of your clothes. Hurry now, before the men come in."

Lena picked up both her dolls from the sofa, and clutching them to her chest, ran out of the room, not even pausing to say goodbye to Nettie. Mrs. Remple hurried after her.

Nettie looked out the window where the street was still teeming with soldiers and horses. No matter what Mrs. Remple said, she would not go across the street while the soldiers were there. Then she heard the sound of stomping feet and realized the men putting their horses in the barn would soon come in. Terrified, she ran for the door, through the dining room, and into the kitchen.

Lena was underneath the work table, a doll in each arm. Maria, the Russian cook, rapidly chopped vegetables above her head. Nettie thought she was making soup for the crowd of soldiers coming in.

"Nettie!" exclaimed Lena. "You must go home before they come."

"I can't go out the front door," Nettie whispered, kneeling down beside her friend. "There are soldiers everywhere."

"But how will you get home?"

"I'll wait till the street is empty," said Nettie. "I'll hide behind the mulberry bushes."

"Your mother will be worried," said Lena. "I know!" She leaned forward. "We'll telephone her and tell her you will stay here till it's safe."

Even in her fear, Nettie smiled. "Silly. We don't have a telephone."

Lena turned pink. As the mill owners, the Remples were much wealthier than their neighbours. They were one of the few families in the village with a telephone.

Suddenly the noise in the other room grew louder. Thumps sounded on the kitchen door, then it was flung open. Maria stepped sideways as she turned around, her wide black skirt hiding the door from the view of the girls under the table. "There are twelve of us here," Nettie heard a man say. "We'll wait in the front room for the meal."

"I'm afraid of the soldiers," Lena whispered to Nettie. "I'm afraid they'll kill us."

Nettie wanted to say she wasn't afraid, but the words didn't come.

The girls sat under the table in silence, listening to the comforting sounds around them: soup bubbling on the stove, the thud of Maria's knife as the onions, cabbage, and potatoes were chopped. They could smell the soup too, mixing with the yeasty scent of bread cooling on the table.

The kitchen door opened again and the girls leaned towards each other. This time Maria was stirring the soup and there was no one to step between them and the soldiers.

But it was Lena's mother. She spotted the girls under the table immediately. "Lena, what are you doing hiding under the table? Nettie! Why are you still here?"

Nettie crawled out and stood up. "I didn't want to go out in the street when the soldiers were there," she explained in a small voice. "I'll go home now." She rushed to the back door before Mrs. Remple could tell her to leave again.

"That would be best," said Mrs. Remple. "You will be fine, I'm sure."

I'm not sure, thought Nettie. Today, Mrs. Remple seemed almost as frightening as the soldiers, though, so she hugged her shawl around herself and opened the door.

It was chilly outside, for it had been a cloudy, rainy day, and now it was almost dark. Nettie could hear sounds of men and horses as she stepped into the garden. She stayed as far from the stables and the mill as she could, clinging closely to the sides of the house where she thought she would be less likely to meet anyone. Every shadow looked like a soldier, but nothing stopped her passage around the house.

Once she reached the front, she was relieved to see that there were far fewer soldiers on the street than before. They must have found places to stay, she guessed, and hoped that none were at her house.

Feeling braver now there were not so many soldiers and none close, Nettie stepped away from the bushes surrounding the Remple house and into the street. Glancing quickly both ways, she darted across the street, not breathing until she was in the shadows of the familiar bushes.

It was quiet in the schoolyard, with no sign that soldiers or horses had stepped into the yard. Do they only go to rich people's homes? Nettie wondered, relieved. She ran quickly past the school and up to the door of the house.

The welcoming smell of frying sausages met Nettie as she let herself in. She glanced around quickly. Papa sat against the big stove, warming his back as he liked to do. Sara's knife paused over the round loaf of rye bread and Jacob laid down his newspaper.

Everyone looked at Nettie.

"Nettie," cried Mama. "Are you all right?"

"Yes, Mama." She hung up her shawl and washed her hands in the basin. "There are soldiers at the Remples."

"What are they doing?" asked Jacob. "Did you see them?"

"I only saw the soldiers in the street," said Nettie. She went over and hugged her father who looked worried. "Lena and I went to the kitchen while the soldiers put their horses in the barn."

"Well," said Mama, "I'm glad Lena's mother had the sense to keep you there till now. I was worried she might send you home while those men were everywhere. You could hardly have made it across the street without being stepped on."

Nettie nodded her head silently and hoped that Lena would not have reason to be afraid of the soldiers staying with them.

Later they learned that all the soldiers stayed in homes throughout the village. No one had a choice, the soldiers stayed where they pleased.

In the morning some of the soldiers went door to door demanding firearms.

When they came to her house, Nettie's father answered the door. "We don't have any guns or rifles," he told the soldiers. He stepped backwards as they pushed past him into the house.

Jacob was already away to Woelks' for the day, but Nettie, Sara, and Mama were in the kitchen. When they heard the soldier's voice, they all froze where they stood. Nettie, standing by the door, could see what was happening. Mama motioned her to step back, but Nettie's feet were too heavy to lift.

"Come, come," the soldier replied in Russian. "We know there was a self-defence unit here. We know you welcomed the German army here. We know they left rifles behind. Bring them out or we will take you to our commander."

"I have no rifles," said Papa again. He held himself stiffly straight and his voice didn't waver. "I have never shot a gun and I don't own any."

"We will see," said the soldier. He nodded to his men. Immediately four of them started searching through the house. They went into the attic, they looked behind doors and in cupboards and under beds. They came back to the front room, their hands empty.

"All right," said the superior soldier. "You may remain here for now. If we find you've lied to us..."

They went to every house in the village. Nettie heard afterwards that they had found four shotguns and two rifles. They didn't find any of the German rifles. What had happened to them?

When the soldiers finally left, they took the guns with them. They also took many of the village horses. They didn't buy the horses, but told the owners it was their duty as Russian citizens to support the government. No one in the village said they didn't want the new Russian government, they just let the men lead away their horses. Some of the soldiers left their tired horses behind, but most of the soldiers rode away on one horse, leading the other.

At school Nettie learned that the father of one of her classmates was also required to obey the soldiers.

"They took your father?" demanded a boy. "Will he join the Red Army now?"

Tina Krahn shook her head, tears standing in her eyes. "They said he could come back when he had delivered the food to the army camp. He has our ladder wagon and two of our horses. It's filled with food they took from different people."

It was mostly the farmers like Tina's father who had their food taken, Nettie knew. Most of the houses in the village belonged to farmers. Their barns were joined to the house so they could feed the animals without going outside. They stored grain and extra food in the attic. Whether the strangers at the door were robbers openly stealing or soldiers saying they were protecting the people, they all knew there would be food in the attic of any Mennonite farmer's home.

CHAPTER 16

June 25, 1919. There are robbers in town almost every day. Sometimes there are just two or three looking for something to eat or some clothes to steal. Sometimes there are dozens riding through with their black flag waving. The worst is at night when they bang on the doors while people sleep.

The hammering on the door echoed through the house.

Nettie heard movement from her parents' room. Then there was a rustle in her own room. Nettie shrank closer to Sara, trying to disappear.

"Quickly, girls," whispered Mama. "Get dressed. If they come in here, we must be ready."

Ready for what, Nettie wondered. To hide? To climb out the window?

As she pulled her dress over her head, Nettie heard Papa open the door in the other room. There was the familiar sound of heavy boots and coarse voices.

"Where do you keep your treasures?" demanded the voice.

"We have no treasures," said Papa. "I am a teacher. We just have enough to eat."

"A teacher!" Nettie heard people move around in the other room. Then she heard heavy thumps. They were throwing Papa's books on the floor! "Make sure you teach the right language," the man said. Nettie heard ripping sounds. "No more of this German garbage." There were more thumps and bangs. "Come, let's go somewhere else."

Amazingly, the men left.

Nettie, Sara, and her mother crept out of the bedroom. There were books all over the front-room floor. Some were ripped. Papa slowly bent down and picked one up. He dusted it with his hand and put it back on the shelf.

"Oh, Papa," cried Nettie. "They ripped your books."

"They didn't hurt us," said Papa.

The thieves stopped at Peter and Liese's house too. They took clothes from Peter and quilts from their bed. Another time, bandits used their knives and slit two of the pillows Liese and Peter had received for wedding gifts. Nettie helped Liese stuff the feathers back inside and sew the pillows shut with tiny, neat stitches.

Each night Nettie lay in bed listening to the sounds outside, afraid to go to sleep in case the robbers came back.

One July day, Nettie realized they had not seen any bandits for over a week.

"Denikin's Army has pushed Makhno to the north," Jacob excitedly told Sara and Nettie. "Probably Abram is there, doing just what he set out to do, protect the Mennonites from the anarchists."

"Yes," said Sara slowly. "But where are the Bolsheviks? Where's the Red Army? Aren't they just as bad?"

"Oh, they're fighting someone else now; it's Denikin who's in control of Ukraine. You'll see, life will go back to normal."

It seemed that Jacob was right, for the peace extended into the fall. They picked the pears and apples off the trees, dug the potatoes from the garden, and school started in the building attached to Nettie's house.

Nettie's father had not completely recovered from his illness. Listening to Mama and Liese talk while they cut up fruit to dry, Nettie learned for the first time that her father had suffered from several small strokes. It affected the way the right side of his body worked. He was determined to continue teaching, however, and tried to force his arm and leg to work just as they had always done. This effort made him so tired that each day after school he made his way cautiously to the bench in the front room, where he stayed till bedtime, warming his back against the stove. Often he spent the night there too, wrapped in a warm quilt.

Nettie still cleaned the schoolroom while Sara wrote the next day's assignments on the chalkboard. When

Sara cared for the Warkentin children while their mother was sick, Nettie wrote the assignments on the board. She painstakingly wrote her neatest, not wanting the other students to see messy writing.

One day after her work in the schoolroom, Mama sent Nettie to tidy the front room. She dusted the furniture and rearranged her tea set and the photographs on the china cabinet. As she worked, she occasionally glanced at her father, sitting so still. Though he held a book, in all the time she was there she didn't see him turn a single page.

Jacob helped with harvest. The Communist government had taken away much of the farmers' land and given it to the Ukrainian peasants, but each Mennonite farmer still had some. Because so many of the horses had been stolen, or "requisitioned" as the Red Army called it, the farmers had to work together. They took turns with what animals were left to pull the wagons and machinery. Jacob worked for anyone who needed his help, receiving grain or flour as payment. He put the bags in the attic so the family could eat in the winter.

There was always more work to do in the autumn. Nettie and Mama kept busy preparing for the winter, with Sara helping whenever she was home. Often Liese came over to work with them as they cut apples or pears to dry or boiled watermelon juice for syrup. She always took some back so she and Peter would have food to eat in the winter. Nettie usually walked back to Liese's house with her, carrying things.

Liese and Peter lived in a small house, but even so there was another couple who lived with them, Henry and Hilda Woelk. Henry and Hilda's house had been burned down by bandits. One day Nettie helped Liese by laying apples out on the screens on the veranda roof to dry in the sun.

"Don't put them too close together," Liese warned, "or they won't dry properly."

"I know," said Nettie. "I've helped Mama."

Liese smiled. "Of course. I'm just frustrated because I want to do it myself."

She didn't do it herself because Peter didn't want her to climb. The baby was due soon and she had to take care of herself.

While she laid the newly cut apples on the screen, Nettie removed the dry apples from previous days. She put these into a bowl which she carefully handed to Liese before she climbed down.

"These look good," Liese said. She chose a small piece of apple and popped it into her mouth before checking through the bowl to see that all the apples were dry enough.

"I have to go home now," said Nettie reluctantly.

"Why don't you stay and have supper with Peter and me?" asked Liese. "Henry and Hilda are visiting Hilda's family today, so they won't be here."

"I'll ask Mama," said Nettie eagerly. "I'm sure she won't mind."

"I'll expect you back right away," said Liese, smiling as she turned to go into the house.

Moments later, Nettie burst into the kitchen where Mama was checking the potatoes. "Mama, Liese invited me to have supper with them," she said in a rush. "Please say I may."

"And what do I do with all the food I've made?" asked Mama, looking up.

"You and Papa and Sara will eat it," Nettie said. "And Jacob will eat the rest when he gets back from the farm."

"That's fine, then, but change your apron first, you have apple stains all over it."

Nettie quickly changed her apron, grabbed her shawl for when she came home, and hurried back to Liese's.

She knocked on Liese's door, but there was no answer. She stepped inside. The room was dim and shadowy.

"Liese?" called Nettie. "Liese, where are you?"

She stepped further into the house. There was no sign that Liese had started preparing supper. Liese herself was nowhere in sight

Nettie felt suddenly sick in her stomach. Where could Liese be?

Then Nettie noticed the trap door leading to the cellar was open. She stepped closer and peeked down.

Darkness. With trembling hands, Nettie went to the table and lit the lamp. She carried it back to the trap door and took a tentative step downwards.

In the light of the lamp, Nettie could see Liese in a crumpled heap at the bottom of the stairs.

CHAPTER 17

September 22, 1919. Liese's baby died when she fell down the stairs, but Liese will get better. She is sad. Peter is sad too. All the babies in my life have died, first Mama's and now Liese's. People should stop having babies because they always die.

"Abram is sick," Mama told Nettie. "He's in Chortitza with typhus. Your papa and I must bring him home."

Nettie didn't know what typhus was, but she wasn't worried. Mama could nurse anyone back to health. "But Mama," said Nettie, thinking of something else. "How can you bring him home? We don't have a wagon or a horse and we have no money to pay for them."

"We'll sell some flour," said Mama. "Jacob has earned flour and so has your papa. We'll trade the flour and then we can go to Abram."

Mama went on forming the bun dough into perfect *tweiback*. Nettie went to the barn to find Jacob.

"My flour!" exclaimed Jacob. His voice was angry. He leaned the fork against the wall and stared at Nettie. "I earned that flour for us to eat, not for Mama and Papa to go chasing after Abram, who shouldn't have gone away in the first place." He picked up the fork and stabbed it into the hard dirt floor. "If they were just going to throw it away like that, I should have kept it. I could have bought a horse with that flour."

Nettie watched Jacob in silence. Did he think he could buy a horse with two bags of flour? Who had a horse to sell anyway, with so many horses stolen or taken for the war? Jacob pulled the fork out of the floor and started pitching hay for the cows. He continued muttering angrily to himself. Nettie crept out of the barn without Jacob even noticing.

Papa was not sitting in his usual spot by the stove. Nettie guessed he was making arrangements to use someone's horse and wagon.

Mama packed *tweiback* and cheese. She took a mattress for the floor of the wagon and a pile of quilts. Early the next morning she and Papa climbed onto the wagon and drove out of the village towards Chortitza.

Bernhard Mathies took Papa's place in the grade five and six classroom. He had a grey beard and grey hair. Nettie guessed he was so old that he must have been a teacher when her father was in school. She was glad he wasn't listening to her lessons.

Sara was gone most days, taking care of the Warkentin children. Jacob was away too, helping farmers with their harvest or gathering hay for their own cows.

The Kroeger clock ticked loudly in the emptiness of the house. When it bonged on the hour, Nettie jumped.

Each morning Nettie filled the big stove with fuel to keep the house warm. She made breakfast for Jacob, then gathered the eggs and fed the hens while Jacob milked the cows. Nettie tried to milk, but her hands were still too small to get all the milk. It was important that it be done in time to meet the herdsman before he took the cows to the pasture. After school was the loneliest time. Then Nettie visited Liese or invited Lena over to play with their paper dolls.

Nettie buttered a slice of bread after school one day in October, then sat in Mama's rocking chair to eat it. She didn't have to make supper, for both Sara and Jacob were away. Jacob was working in another village and didn't think he would be home that day at all. Sara could not leave the Warkentin children till their father returned later that evening.

There was a loud thumping of feet outside and Jacob burst into the house. His face was red and he was breathing hard.

"Jacob!" Nettie exclaimed. "What's wrong? Why are you home so soon?"

"They've come back. Makhno, he's come back. They came to Friesens' during the night." Nettie was horrified to see that Jacob had tears in his eyes. "They killed —" He stopped speaking and dropped into a chair. Nettie stared at Jacob, unable to speak, feeling as if her insides were frozen.

Jacob took several deep breaths, and then he started speaking again, more slowly. "They rode into the village during the night, waking all the people. They stole things just like in the spring, but then they ordered some people to carry straw into their houses and set them on fire. When anyone refused, they —" Jacob stopped and covered his face with his hands.

"When I got there this morning," Jacob went on, his voice barely more than a whisper, "the Friesens' house was gone. There was nothing left but the big brick stove. There were other houses burned too. Three or four of them. Most of the people had run away, but Hans was still there." Hans was the Friesens' oldest son. He and Jacob had roomed together when they were away at school. "I helped him make coffins for his father and his uncle, then I came home."

Nettie made tea for Jacob, and gave him cheese and bread. Not knowing what else to do, she sat down and watched him. After a long time Jacob got up. He washed his face and hands, then sat down again and took a bite. Putting the bread down, he looked at Nettie.

"Mama and Papa," he said hoarsely. "What if they meet them on the road?"

For the rest of the afternoon, Jacob, who was always doing something, who never wanted to sit still, sat and stared at the wall. The next morning he didn't go away to work. "I need to gather feed for our own cows," he said. And Nettie, wishing she could help Jacob, went to school and learned Russian grammar.

CHAPTER 18

October 16, 1919. Mama and Papa brought Abram home safely. They did not get stopped by bandits. Abram is much thinner and has no hair. Mama said she cut it off because of the lice. I didn't see any lice, so I guess Mama got them all. He doesn't talk or eat. He just lies with his eyes closed and drinks the broth Mama feeds him.

Nettie peeked into her bedroom. Abram lay on her bed, sleeping, huddled under the quilts as if he was cold. His cheeks were caved in and his eyes seemed to have sunk deeper into his head. She pulled the door shut and tiptoed away.

In the kitchen, Mama was putting fresh *tweiback* on the table to cool. Sara and Liese both sat nearby, sewing.

"Are you sure that's Abram?" asked Nettie. "He doesn't look like himself at all."

"He has been very sick," said Mama. "But yes, I am sure." She laid the last *tweiback* on the table and then paused, her hand hovering in the air.

"It was terrible, there in the school in Chortitza. There were no tables or chairs, they had burned them all to keep warm. Instead, there were rows of men lying on the floor. Some of them were sleeping like the dead, others were yelling and calling for people who weren't there. There were no nurses to care for them, and only two doctors in all of Chortitza. They were dirty, but there was no water to wash with and very little to drink. No medicine. Hardly any food. Lice on everyone. That Makhno, he has much to answer for." She set the pan down with a bang, then spoke again, more softly.

"It was hard, then, to tell which one was my son. They were all sons, someone's sons, and now they were lying there on the floor in that cold building." Her voice broke, and she threw her apron up over her face. Her shoulders shook. Nettie stepped back, horrified, but Liese rose and gently led Mama out of the room.

Nettie looked at Sara.

"Put some water on to boil," said Sara. "Mama will want tea."

Nettie didn't see her mother break down again. During the first days, Mama did all Abram's nursing herself, not letting anyone else into the girls' bedroom where he slept, lest they get the disease as well. As time went by, she let Sara help her change his bedding and Liese sit in the room to keep Abram company.

"Is he going to sleep forever, Mama?" asked Nettie. She watched her mother as she spun silk strands into thread on the spinning wheel. "He's been home two weeks. Shouldn't he be better by now?"

"What's the matter? Don't you like sleeping on the *schloapbenjk?*"

"I don't mind Abram sleeping in my bed. I just thought he should be getting better."

"The typhus is a bad disease," said Mama. "We must be glad Abram is alive. He will get well in time."

"Will he talk again when he's better?" asked Nettie.

Mama stopped spinning and stared at Nettie. "Of course he will talk again. The disease didn't hurt his voice."

"But he doesn't talk now."

"No, he is too weak. And maybe he is too upset by what he saw when he was away."

"What was that, Mama?" asked Nettie. "What did he see?"

"War is not gentle," said Mama. She reached out and hugged Nettie.

"Soldiers carry guns," Mama went on. "Guns kill people. Abram shouldn't have been there. I'm sure he saw things that went against what we believe. It will take Abram a long time to get over that."

"What did he see?" persisted Nettie. She pulled away and looked at her mother. Mama avoided her eyes, turning back to her spinning wheel.

"I don't know," she said. "He was even sicker when we found him than he is now. He said things that made no sense. We'll have to wait till he's better, then maybe he will tell us about when he was gone. Now, go gather the eggs before dark."

Nettie gathered the eggs, then went back to peek into her bedroom.

She could barely see Abram in the dim light of early evening.

"Abram," she whispered. "Are you feeling better?"

"Hungry," he said. Nettie could barely make out the word.

"I'll tell Mama," said Nettie. "She'll give you food."

"He's hungry!" exclaimed Mama, after Nettie told her the news. "That's wonderful. But he must not eat too much, or he will get sicker. I'll bring him some broth."

He'd rather have *tweiback*, thought Nettie. She took one herself and ate small bites as she watched her mother heat the soup.

The next evening, Abram sat up in bed for a while. The day after, he was on the bench by the stove when Nettie came in from school. He was wrapped in one of Mama's quilts, staring at the empty wall.

Nettie peeked around the corner at him, then backed away.

"He doesn't look like Abram," she whispered to Jacob.

Jacob took a bite out of a roasted bun. "Serves him right," he said when he could talk. Nettie saw that Jacob was still angry about the flour Papa had traded to help get Abram home. Was a horse more important than his own brother? she wondered.

Nettie crept back to peek at Abram again. He hadn't moved.

"Nettie." Mama spoke behind Nettie. "I've heated some broth for Abram. Do you think you can hold the cup while he drinks it?"

Nettie took the cup of steaming liquid carefully in both hands and brought it to her brother.

"Do you want some broth?" she whispered. She couldn't bring herself to talk out loud when Abram was so strange.

Abram didn't move.

Nettie held the cup closer so he could smell the soup and feel the steam.

Abram still didn't move.

"Abram," she whispered. And then a little louder: "Abram!"

He jumped as if she'd startled him. He slowly turned his head till he was looking at her. "Nettie."

Relief flooded through Nettie. He knew her. She blinked hurriedly to keep from crying. Smiling shakily, she held the cup to his mouth.

Abram leaned forward slightly and Nettie tilted the cup. He took a small sip and a few drops dripped on the quilt.

"Do you want to hold it yourself?" asked Nettie.

Abram shook his head slightly and leaned forward for another sip. Slowly, a sip at a time, he drank half the cup before leaning back and closing his eyes. Nettie studied him for a moment, looking for something familiar in his thin face and hairless head.

"He's not getting any fatter," she told her mother as she handed her the cup.

"Don't worry, little one." Her mother's voice was reassuring. "He will get better quickly now, you will see."

Liese came almost every day to sit with Abram. Being with him seemed to help her get over some of the sadness of losing her baby.

One day when Nettie came home from school, she found Mama, Liese, and Sara all sitting with Abram.

Abram was speaking. Nettie tiptoed to the door of the front room and listened.

"I joined the Volunteers," he said. "I thought they would keep out the Red Army." He paused, and covered his eyes for a moment. "I thought the Whites would be the honourable army, trying to do what was right." He shook his head. "There is no honourable army." He sipped from a glass of water, then set it down. "We were resting in a Ukrainian village for a few days when I got sick."

"What happened when you got sick?" Liese asked gently. "What did you do?"

"They left me there," said Abram. "A peasant woman cared for me. The army had thought I had typhus, but I didn't. I got better soon and was going to come home, but before I could..." His listeners all waited.

"The Red Army came into the village. They ate and slept in the peasants' homes and when they left in the morning, they took me with them."

"But did they know you were a White Army soldier?" exclaimed Nettie, unable to keep silent.

Abram looked at her and smiled faintly. "If they had, they would have shot me," he said simply. "They thought I was another peasant. I was wearing clothes that had belonged to the woman's dead husband while she washed my uniform. It saved my life."

"Thank God for that woman," said Mama. She wiped her eyes on a corner of her apron.

"But then you did get typhus," prompted Liese.

"I marched with the Reds for a few weeks. I always looked for a chance to escape, but there was none."

"Were you in any battles?" asked Nettie. "Did you have to shoot a gun?"

Abram closed his eyes and leaned back against the stove.

"That's enough," said Mama. She rose to her feet. "No more questions. Let your brother rest."

CHAPTER 19

December 5, 1919. Two boys died of typhus. They were brothers and just little. Sara's choir sang at the funeral. There are many funerals. We do not say much about Christmas, but I am working on a new Wish to give to Papa and Mama. I cannot write it on the special paper, for there is no paper left.

Nettie thought every bandit passing through Gruenfeld stopped at Lena's house. It was the biggest house in the village, so it looked to be the most likely place to find things worth stealing. It didn't take many visits from the robbers before there was nothing at the Remples' left to steal.

"They've taken all Mama's linen," Lena told Nettie after one of these terrifying visits in the night. "We sleep on the feather ticks now, with no sheets and only the oldest blankets. Papa has almost no clothes left. Mama hid his winter coat and a few other things under the straw in the attic, so they haven't found them, but every robber that comes takes a pair of trousers, or a shirt or a jacket. If they can't find clothes in the wardrobe, they demand Papa take off the clothes he's wearing. They point their swords at him and demand his clothes, and Mama says, "Give them to him, Herman, or they will kill you."

"Maybe they will stop coming to your house now there's nothing left to steal," suggested Nettie.

Unfortunately the bandits didn't think about how many others had been before them. When they found nothing to steal, they became angry.

"They broke my china dolls," Lena told Nettie another day, tears pouring down her face. "One of the men broke the door on the china cabinet with his pistol. Then he stuck his arm in and swept everything onto the floor. Everything smashed — Mama's teapot, her special dishes, both my china dolls..."

It seemed the robbers knew that teachers were not wealthy. Or maybe it was because their house was less noticeable, joined to the school as it was. Sometimes men demanded Mama cook a meal for them, and once a group of drunken robbers asked for money. Mama told them that Papa was a teacher who had not been paid in many months. She gave them a few rubles and some freshly made *tweiback*, and though they cursed and swore, they left and went somewhere else.

Everyone in the village had to feed the bandits. "After they ate our supper," Tina told Nettie at school one day, "they went into the storeroom and threw all the jars of food outside. Mama and I had bottled so many cherries and so much watermelon syrup and they just threw it on the ground, breaking the window and breaking all the bottles."

"But why didn't they take it to eat?" demanded Nettie, confused by this waste of food.

"Papa says they don't think about the future," Tina said. Her father had returned safely to the village after his trip to the Red Army with the wagonload of food. Though he came back with his own wagon, they had kept his good horses and given him a team of old, worn-out horses. It didn't matter, though, for soon afterwards robbers took the old horses and the wagon away. At least Tina's father was safe.

Other people were not so lucky. Some people couldn't stand seeing robbers come into their homes. Johann Schroeder's grandmother didn't understand why her son was letting the strange men steal her embroidered pillowcases and crocheted tablecloths. She stepped forward to stop them and one of the men pushed her aside with his sword, cutting deeply into her arm and her side. When Mr. Schroeder protested, another man shot him in the head. Mrs. Schroeder took her family away to a village she thought was safer. Johann did not come back to school, not even to say goodbye.

His was not the only family to leave. When Lena and Nettie crept into an empty house, they found bits of broken furniture, torn curtains, and holes in the walls. Even the windows were broken. Most horrifying of all were the dark brown stains on the floors.

"Will the families come back when the robbers are gone?" Nettie wondered. No one knew the answer.

Then came the day Lena's father pulled out his last wagon, an old, weathered one that the bandits hadn't thought worth stealing. He loaded it with what little was left in their house. Then he came across the street to the Pauls' house.

"We're going to the Crimea," Mr. Remple told Nettie's parents. "They've taken everything we had. We must go before we lose our lives as well."

While Papa and Mr. Remple solemnly kissed each other's cheeks, Nettie grabbed her shawl and ran out of the house.

Lena stood by the wagon watching as Nettie ran across the street.

Nettie stopped in front of Lena, suddenly shy. What could she say? Her friend was leaving; she might be killed as she travelled, and even if she made it safely to the Crimea, they would probably never see each other again.

I don't want you to go was on the tip of Nettie's tongue, but how could she say it when staying was so dangerous?

"Bandits came again last night," Lena said. "We had no oil for the lamps, so they used matches. They walked through our house, looking for things to steal. They dropped the matches everywhere. Mama and Papa walked behind, putting out the fires. I want to go where there are no bandits."

"I want you to be safe," said Nettie. That was what she really wanted. How could Lena be safe in Gruenfeld where their house was an invitation to every bandit that came through?

"Get in the wagon," came the voice of Mr. Remple from across the street. Nettie turned and saw him coming out of the schoolyard, one of Mama's quilts in his arms. "Lena, help your brothers. Do you have the blankets? Look, Mrs. Pauls sent this warm quilt as a gift. Lena, wrap it around yourself and your brothers."

Lena's youngest brother came running out of the house, bundled up in a hat and coat. Nettie helped him into the wagon, then stepped back. Lena climbed up beside the two younger boys and wrapped the quilt securely around them. This done, she looked back at Nettie.

"I'll miss you," Lena said, her voice low.

"Me too," said Nettie. She stepped forward and reached her hand up to Lena. Lena clasped her fingers tightly, letting go only when her father had seated himself on the wooden bench beside her mother and picked up the reins. Nettie stepped backwards, out of the way. Glancing around, she discovered that a small crowd of people had joined her to say goodbye to the Remples.

Together they watched the wagon until it disappeared from sight. Then Nettie walked slowly back across the street to her home. There Mama sat on the seat by the big stove, warming her back, her fingers briskly knitting a sock for Abram.

In only a few days, Lena's home looked like the ones that Nettie and Lena had crept into just weeks before. Windows broken, carpets ripped up, furniture gone. Nettie tried not to look in that direction when she walked outside.

This became easier as winter settled on the village. Snow covered the yards and lodged in the branches of the bushes and trees. It also hid much of the damage from the bandits. School continued, but with fewer students. So many families had left; others could not afford to pay for their children to go to school.

Jacob was restless. He shovelled paths through the snow from the street to the school and from the school to the house. He shovelled paths for Liese and for old Mrs. Guenther and the Klassen family next door. Now that he no longer had farm work to do for others, he took care of the cows at home. He brought in the straw for the big central stove and helped Mama clean out the ashes. When he could find nothing else to do, he visited his friends.

Abram, who had so seldom been at home before he joined the army, now rarely left the house. He refused to go to church with the family on Sunday and never met with his friends in the evenings. He didn't even visit Liese, though she still came to see him.

"He just sits all day," Nettie whispered to Sara as they washed dishes one winter evening. "He doesn't even read."

"He was very sick," said Sara. "He's still recovering."

Mama treated Abram as if he were still sick. She brought him hot drinks. She made as many of his favourite dishes as she had ingredients for. She tried to wrap him in quilts as he sat on the bench by the stove but Abram brushed them away impatiently.

The house was too quiet.

"Let's sing," demanded Nettie. She opened her mouth and out popped the first song that came to mind. *"Stille Nacht, heilige Nacht, Alles schläft, einsam wacht.* Silent Night, Holy Night, All is calm, All is bright."

"Christmas is next week," said Sara. "I'd almost forgotten." She joined in on the next line and the two finished the dishes before the song was done.

"Sing another," said Mama. She was seated at the table, the lamp drawn close as she mended one of Nettie's aprons. "I like to hear your voices."

Mama joined in the next song, and by the end of the first verse, Papa was singing too. Abram turned his head to watch them as they sang, but if Nettie hadn't suddenly decided to surprise him with a hug, she wouldn't have known that his eyes were wet with tears.

CHAPTER 20

January 11, 1920. Uncle Wilhelm came today. We haven't seen him since Liese's wedding. He told us the bandits killed almost everyone in Muensterberg and other villages near there. It happened in November but we didn't hear because people don't travel so much anymore.

"If I could," declared Jacob, "I would fight against that Makhno."

His mother's already stricken face turned even whiter. "But no, Jacob. There is already too much fighting. It's time for peace."

"So we just stand and wait for them to come and kill us, like they did..." Jacob's voice broke but he pressed on. "Like they did Hans Friesen's father and uncle? Uncle Wilhelm, shouldn't we be fighting these anarchists?"

"We tried that last year," said Uncle Wilhelm with a heavy sigh. He fingered his bushy beard. "And look what happened. Last spring the Red Army killed everyone they could find who had been part of the self-defence units." His eyes moved to Abram, who was leaning against the door frame, listening silently. "And there is talk, though I have no proof, that Makhno, he goes harder on the villages where the self–defence units were active."

"So we sit and let them come in, burn our homes, and kill us."

"Now, Jacob. You are young. This terror can't go on forever. The army will crush the Makhnovites."

"Which army? There are three of them in Ukraine right now."

"So you listen to the politics?" Uncle Wilhelm leaned back in his chair. "What do you think will happen?"

"Lenin and his Red Army will crush us all." It was Abram answering, not Jacob. Nettie thought everyone looked at him as if they'd forgotten he could talk.

"Ach, we are far from Moscow. They'll forget about us in a while and we can go back to our old ways. Besides, Denikin is still leading the White forces. They are showing strength."

Papa shook his head. "I wish you were right, Wilhelm, but I fear the Red Army. It's too big. Too well organized."

"Don't forget." Abram's voice was quiet. "Don't forget we grow food here. An army needs food. Ukraine can feed all of Russia. They aren't going to let us go.

Look at how quickly Russia came back into Ukraine when the Germans left."

"Food!" said Mama, as if it was a new thought. "Quickly, Nettie. Peel potatoes. Sara, put water on to boil. We, too, must eat."

Nettie listened to the rest of the conversation while she helped Mama and Sara prepare the evening meal. All the news was bad.

February 4, 1920. Mama had another baby. Sara holds the baby and sings. The baby's name is Frieda.

Nettie opened the door to the midwife. Sara bustled out of the back bedroom where Mama was resting. "You're just in time," she said. "Come with me."

Nettie stared at the door that Sara had shut so firmly, then started as Papa spoke behind her. "You can read to us," he said. "You need to practise your Russian."

"Russian!" exclaimed Nettie, turning slowly towards Papa. "I'd rather read German."

"That's why you will read in Russian," said Papa slowly. "Come, Jacob, Abram, you can listen."

So they all gathered around the kitchen table. Jacob got out his almost-finished harness, Papa whittled slowly, and Abram stared at the wall. Nettie read to them from the history of Russia. She stumbled over words, but seldom did anyone comment or correct her. She was vaguely aware of sounds coming from the bedroom, but only when she heard the unmistakable cry of a baby did Nettie close the book. Papa did not speak, but a slight smile crossed his face. Even Abram looked interested. A few minutes later Sara came out of the bedroom with a bundle of blankets.

"Meet your new daughter, Mr. Pauls," she said formally as she showed the bundle to her father. Nettie rushed around the table to see the new baby. A tiny, round, red face nestled among the white blankets. Her dark eyes seemed to look right at Nettie.

"My sister," Nettie whispered. "My baby sister." She was so happy, she could feel it inside herself, filling her whole body with joy.

March 12, 1920. Four Red soldiers were here yesterday demanding that Mama make them supper. We fed them fried potatoes and noodle soup. They wanted meat but we have none left. They ate all the food, then slept on our floor for the night. Jacob has been sleeping in the barn, guarding the cows, but last night Abram did too. Till now, Mama made him sleep in the living room in the schloapbenjk. She said he was too sick and it was too cold. Not too cold for Jacob, I guess. Baby Frieda smiles at me.

The family heard little news of battles during the winter. People said the White Army had gone into the Crimea until the weather warmed up. Papa continued to teach at school. Nettie thought he was getting better. His right leg still dragged, but walking didn't look like such hard work as it had before. Though he still wrote with his left hand, he used his right arm for small tasks.

The coming of spring brought work for Abram and Jacob. Seeding was more difficult with so many horses gone, either stolen by Makhno's army or requisitioned by Lenin's. Those that were left had to be shared by everyone if the crops were to be planted. Some of the farmers didn't have seed. As with the horses, so much grain had been taken by the armies and the thieves.

Nettie sat in her desk in the school. Looking out the window she could see the flowers on the pear trees. Spring was her favourite time of year. After school Nettie helped Sara in her flower beds. The tulips were already blooming, and violets were coming up around them. The weeds were growing too, but after so many years of helping, Nettie recognized most of them. She enjoyed pulling them up while they were still tiny, leaving room for the flowers to grow big and strong.

Mama let them bring Frieda outside. She lay on a quilt beside them, watching the clouds while her sisters worked in the warm soil.

NOT EVERYTHING THAT CAME IN THE SPRING was good. The news from Chortitza was bad. Most of Makhno's army had spent the winter in Chortitza and the villages around it that made up the colony of Chortitza. They had forced the residents to feed and house them through the many months. In return they shared their lice and typhus with the villagers. Hundreds of people in the colony got the disease that had made Abram so sick. When everyone was sick, who was left to care for them? Because of the many raids, there was little food left. The bandits demanded eggs and milk, even though they had already killed the chickens and cows for meat. Without food, sick people got sicker. People died in almost every family.

In the spring, when the people in the other villages heard the news, they sent what they could to help. Many orphaned children were taken to live in other colonies.

Nettie couldn't imagine how the children felt. First their parents were dead, then they had to move many *versts* away to live with people they'd never met.

Nettie thought of Abram and his rescue months before. If their parents had not brought him home, would he have been one of the dead in Chortitza?

She was grateful that all her family was still alive.

The newest member of the family was growing bigger and crankier every day. Nettie was obliged to rock Frieda after school and in the evenings. As she rocked, she thought of little Johann, who'd also been fussy. Frieda's crying was different, though — stronger, maybe even angry.

"You are going to live," Nettie whispered to her as she rocked the wooden cradle. "You're going to be strong and grow to be a big girl." Frieda stopped crying, gazing at Nettie with her dark eyes.

There were people working the mill again, Ukrainians from a nearby village. The mill wasn't operating every day, but it was often enough that people could take their grain to be ground into flour. One rainy day when Jacob and Abram couldn't work, they took all the grain left in the attic across to the mill, later bringing home bags of flour. Nettie was comforted by the sight of the flour in their attic. There were no hams or sausages left, but the hens were laying.

The garden was growing, and already there had been fresh vegetables for soup.

Jacob and Abram still slept in the barn, but few bandits came to Gruenfeld these days, and none stopped in the school barn. If they had, Nettie wondered, what could Abram and Jacob have done anyway?

As spring turned into summer, soldiers became a common sight. Long lines of uniformed men passed through town, along with wagons full of guns, ammunition, and cannons. Once Nettie saw what Papa told her was an armoured vehicle. Another strange sight was the airplanes. The first time Nettie saw one, she ran for home, frightened, uncertain of what she'd seen. After that she saw them frequently, but they still frightened her. She heard stories of bombs falling from the flying machines, destroying homes and even villages.

Nothing seemed normal. With hungry soldiers stopping by for meals, Mama and Sara spent hours each day baking bread and cooking meals for them to eat. Nettie sometimes helped, but more often she was in the bedroom, rocking Frieda. Though she was afraid of the soldiers, there were days when she wished she could peel potatoes or chop cabbage. She was so tired of rocking the cradle. When I grow up and have a baby, she decided, I will take the rockers off the cradle.

CHAPTER 21

August 20, 1920. We are alone in our house today. All the soldiers have left the village and no new ones have come. It seems strange to me that soldiers can demand a bed or a meal, and people have to feed them or give them blankets. They never pay and hardly ever say thank you.

"But why should you teach when you don't get paid?" asked Mama. She didn't notice Nettie sitting on the floor in the corner of the room writing in her diary.

"What should I do if I don't teach?"

"It's too difficult."

"I can do it, Anna." Nettie peeked up in time to see Papa lift his right arm. It moved a few inches before it fell to his side again. "If I don't try, my whole body may quit working."

"And if you try too hard, you may kill yourself from strain."

"Oh, Anna," Nettie was surprised to see Papa smiling. "Where is your faith? You worry too much. We should be glad the school is still open here. Many schools are closed now."

"Abram, I'm afraid..."

Mama's voice trailed away. Nettie tried to shrink further into the corner. She had never heard Mama talk like that. And she was sure Mama would not be doing it now, if she knew Nettie was listening.

"The Klassens are talking about emigrating," said Papa. "Henry Bergen too."

Emigrating? Nettie had heard the word before but couldn't remember what it meant.

"Where will they go?" asked Mama. "Is there a country that will let them keep their language and religion?"

"They are looking at America," said Papa. "Men went there this summer, requesting sanctuary."

"But how can *we?*" asked Mama. "We have no money to pay for the trip."

Frieda started to cry, so Nettie didn't hear Papa's answer. Mama stood up hurriedly. "Where are Sara and Nettie? Surely one of them can care for the baby." She rushed out of the room, leaving Papa sitting on the bench by the stove. Nettie waited till she saw Papa's head bend over his book. Then she slowly rose to her feet and tiptoed out of the room.

November 7, 1920. The war is over. Makhno has escaped to France. The White Army has been defeated. Abram says the Bolsheviks will want to control everything we do. They are already closing schools that don't have Russian teachers. Our school is still open, but the central schools in Chortitza haven't recovered from the bandit raids. We are not allowed to have any religion in school, not even a Christmas program like we always did.

There was a Christmas program in the church, though, and the children gave their recitations there. Afterwards, they each received a cookie. Nettie ate hers slowly, savouring every bite.

That cookie was the only special food she had for Christmas that year. It had been a poor year for crops. Fewer crops had been seeded in the spring, and then it had hardly rained. With less to harvest, Abram and Jacob had less work. There was very little food stored in the attic. Fortunately there was some garden produce, though not as much as in other years. While Nettie was in school or rocking Frieda, Mama, Liese, and Sara had filled bottles with watermelon syrup, and chopped apples and plums for drying. There were watermelon and cucumber pickles in the cellar, along with onions, cabbages, and potatoes.

Nettie saw soldiers in the village almost every day. "They're afraid we'll rebel again," said Abram. Nettie stood at the window, looking into the street. Several soldiers had just driven into the village in a wagon. There were two more wagons behind them, empty but for the drivers.

All the men wore the familiar uniforms of the Red Army.

"How can we rebel?" asked Nettie. "We have no guns, we have no soldiers."

"They're just making certain," Abram replied. He got up from his seat by the stove and came to stand beside Nettie. "Ukraine fought against Russia more than any other area," he said slowly. "No Ukrainians want to be part of the new Russian Soviet Republic. That's why the soldiers are still here. You know they're still living in people's houses?"

"Still!" said Nettie. She was horrified. It had been bad enough having soldiers sleeping in people's houses and eating their food during the war. Having them staying on afterwards was a terrible thought. "I'm glad they're not in our house," she said. "They're probably staying at farmers' houses where there's more food."

At that moment there was a loud hammering at the door.

Nettie and Abram looked at each other. There was no expression on Abram's face, but Nettie knew hers looked scared. "It's the soldiers, isn't it?" she whispered.

Abram nodded and moved to the door. Mama and Papa were visiting the Klassens next door and Sara was at choir practice. Nettie stayed out of sight, peeking around the corner just to see what the soldier looked like.

"We are requisitioning flour," said the man at the door. "Two bags from every farmer, one bag from every family that doesn't farm. Do you have any guns or rifles?"

"No," said Abram. "Of course not. We don't have much flour either. There are seven people living here. Our father is a teacher who isn't getting paid. We need all our flour."

"I'm sorry," said the officer. Nettie didn't think he sounded sorry. "The army needs food as well. Are you getting the flour or do I send a man to get it?"

"I'll get it," said Abram. Nettie wondered what Mama would say when she came home and found the army had taken more of their food.

CHAPTER 22

June 27, 1921. No one has work, not even Sara. Every day is hot. It hasn't rained in weeks and the garden seems to be standing still.

Every drop of water used in the house was saved and carried out to the garden. It kept the plants alive, but they hardly grew. There was no water for the flowers, so most of them died. Mama wanted to water more, but the well only gave enough for what they needed to drink and to cook and to wash. Papa thought it would go dry if they used it for the garden.

Fortunately, the mulberry bushes had deep roots. They still grew leaves for the silkworms. Mama and Sara took turns at the spinning wheel, converting twenty thin strands into sewing thread. Mama used this thread for mending. Even Papa had patches on his clothes. When there was extra thread, Mama took it to the market to trade.

Nettie thought she should learn to spin too, but Mama said she was much more useful taking care of Frieda. Frieda needed more care than ever. Nettie didn't have to rock her as much as she used to. But now that Frieda was a year and a half, she was walking on her own and getting into things.

They were on the last bag of flour. There was little left from last fall's garden harvest. The cows gave some milk, but for how much longer when there was no hay to feed them? Each day the Ukrainian herdsman took the village cows to the pasture for the day, bringing them back for evening milking. When there was enough grass in the pasture, the cows didn't eat much hay when they returned to the barn. Now, with the grass in the pasture short and brown and dry, the cows were still hungry when they came back. When Sara milked them, the pail was less than half full.

The hens ran around the schoolyard looking for their own food. Each night Mama locked them in the shed, letting them out after they'd laid their eggs in the morning. There weren't many eggs. There were fewer hens now too. Nettie wondered if someone was stealing them to make soup.

Mama made noodles for supper. They ate them with a little butter.

After supper, Sara and Nettie went to the barn with Jacob, watching as he piled dried grass in front of the two hungry animals. "We need to get rid of one of the cows," said Jacob. "There isn't enough feed for two. If we sold one, we could buy some grain and potatoes."

"If only it would rain," said Nettie, "then our potatoes would grow and we wouldn't need to buy any."

"Everything needs rain," said Jacob. He and Sara looked at each other.

"We could butcher Blossom," suggested Sara.

"She'd be awful tough."

"Soup, stew. We could eat her all winter."

"Then we have to feed her till it's cold enough for the meat to keep."

Nettie didn't want to butcher Blossom, but she didn't want to sell her either. She had been part of their family since Nettie was a little girl. "I'll help gather feed for her," she said.

"We'll talk to Mama," said Sara. "She and Papa will decide."

Nettie was right about potatoes needing rain. The next time she and Sara walked out to the community garden, the tops had already died on the potatoes, weeks earlier than normal. They had come to hoe the weeds, but there were no weeds to hoe. When there is no rain, nothing grows. Instead Sara dug in the ground with her hoe. "These potatoes aren't going to grow any bigger now," she said. "Let's see what's under here."

What was under there was five little potatoes no bigger than walnuts.

"Oh, dear."

They dug till Nettie's apron was filled with the tiny potatoes. Mama looked at them with a slight frown, then said briskly, "Nettie, you wash them. We'll have them for supper with milk gravy."

As the days went by, there was more gravy, but fewer potatoes, in the pot. More often they ate millet soup or noodles.

On July 20, Nettie's twelfth birthday, she was amazed that Mama was able to make one of her favourite meals, *rollküake* and watermelon. The crispy rectangles of the fried *rollküake* tasted wonderful with the sweet juiciness of the ripe watermelon. This melon hadn't grown in the garden outside the village – the vines there were dried and shrivelled – but on one of the vines Nettie had planted in their house garden. There, where they were watered with the wash water from the house, the plants were green and growing, though not as lush as in normal years. The eggs Mama had saved for the *rollküake* were the last eggs the hens laid.

Soon after that, Papa decided they couldn't keep Blossom any longer. Nettie went with Jacob to the market.

No one wanted a cow.

"Guess we'll just have to feed old Blossom a few more months."

Nettie sighed. She didn't know what she wanted. Keep Blossom and spend hours picking bits of dry grass to feed her? Butcher her and have soup with meat in it again? Sell her? She patted the cow's side, feeling the ribs beneath her hand.

"Jacob, Nettie, did you just buy that cow?"

Gerhard Funk ran up to them, his face long and pale. "I'm looking for a cow. Ours died having her calf. I need milk for the children."

Nettie knew Mr. Funk. His wife had died from typhus last winter. Now he had four small children to care for, all of them too young to go to school.

Jacob reached out the hand holding Blossom's rope. "No, sir. We were trying to sell her. We haven't enough feed for her."

"I'm not sure how I'll feed her myself," said Mr. Funk, "but the children need milk." He accepted the rope and stroked Blossom's soft brown head. "Uh, what did you want for her?"

"Do you have any grain?" Gerhard Funk was a farmer. Surely he would have some wheat or rye for flour.

"Some," he said cautiously. "We have potatoes, and I could give you a ham when we butcher the pig this fall. Do you need any watermelon syrup? My mother made so much syrup last year, she filled every bottle in her house, my house, and my sister Ruth's."

"That would be good," said Nettie, when she thought Jacob was hesitating. They were almost out of syrup and the watermelon crop was no better than the potatoes.

Mr. Funk promised to bring over the traded items, then he turned away, leading Blossom.

It felt like Christmas when Mr. Funk brought over the syrup, potatoes, and flour. He brought dried plums too. Nettie was happy to think of eating *pluma moos* again.

"I hope Blossom gives you lots of milk," Nettie said as he left.

"That's her name, is it?" said Mr. Funk. "Good thing you told me. We'll take good care of Blossom."

CHAPTER 23

September 4, 1921. School should have started, but it didn't. Since so little grew, there is almost nothing to harvest. It is strange not to be cutting up bushels of fruit to dry. We don't see Liese very much. Peter's mother is sick, so Liese helps her with her work.

"Everywhere I go they talk of emigrating," exclaimed Nettie's mother when she came in from the market. She had tried to sell her silk thread, but it seemed no one in Gruenfeld needed thread. "Leaving is all they talk about. As if people who can't buy food can afford to move to a new country."

"Where do they want to move to?" asked Nettie. "Germany?"

"*Ach,* no. Germany has too many problems from the war. She can't take more people. No, the people here, they all want to go to America."

"America," repeated Nettie. The very sound of the name was exotic. "But do they speak German there? Or Russian?"

"Some people speak German. Many Mennonites moved there back in the eighteen-seventies. I even know of some who went at the beginning of this century."

"Canada," said Papa. He held his book open in his lap, his finger marking the page. "The people want to go to Canada."

"Canada?" questioned Nettie, wondering if she'd misunderstood her father. "Are there Mennonites in Canada?"

He nodded. "Yes, and they are working to bring more," he said slowly. He turned back to his book.

Nettie looked at her mother. "Will the Mennonites have to speak English in Canada?"

"I don't know." She looked at her husband, but he acted as if he didn't hear. "When the Mennonites moved to Russia more than a hundred years ago, Catherine the Great promised they could keep their own language and their own churches and their own schools. And they told us our sons wouldn't have to fight in the wars."

"But now we learn Russian in our schools," said Nettie, "and they don't let our ministers be teachers anymore." And some of our sons fight in the wars, she added to herself.

"They make promises," said her mother with a sigh. "But when the leaders change, they don't think they need to keep the old promises."

"Will things be better in America, I mean Canada?"

"Who knows?" said her mother. "Who knows? It can't be worse."

But Nettie wondered. Does she really know it can't be worse? It was horrible what people had done to other people in Russia. There had been a time when she would not have believed anyone could be so terrible. How did her mother know that things could not be worse?

The door opened and Sara came in, returning from choir practice. "Everyone says there's food coming," she said before she had even taken off her coat. "From America."

"When does it come?" asked Nettie. She thought of the heavy bread and fried onions that were all she had eaten today. "Is it for everyone? How soon will it get here?"

"Some already arrived at the coast," said Sara, "but the Bolsheviks are keeping it in storehouses. Some people are getting parcels of food sent directly to them. Helen said they received a parcel from her uncle in America. They got canned milk and tea and even meat."

"Do we have relatives in America?"

"None who will send us food," said Mama. She picked up her sewing and held it close to her eyes. "We must do our best and trust God."

"Yes, Mama," said both Sara and Nettie. Later, in bed, Nettie asked Sara to tell her again about the food parcels people had received. She fell asleep dreaming of relatives she'd never met, mailing food across the ocean.

CHAPTER 24

November 20, 1921. Jacob has moved to Steinfeld. He's doing chores for a Mrs. Enns in exchange for food and a place to sleep. He doesn't get paid anything at all, but our food lasts longer. He's already made friends in the village. Abram has to take care of Daisy now. I'm glad. He thinks he can sit all day while other people work.

Every day there was something to eat, but it was never enough. Every day Nettie went to bed hungry.

Several times a week Mama made a loaf of bread from the flour from Mr. Funk. To make it last longer, she added anything she could find that might be edible. "When there's not enough flour, we improvise," she said. One day she looked at the pile of grass and weeds Nettie and Abram had gathered for Daisy. She carried some of the thistles into the house. Nettie followed curiously. Mama rolled the dry thistles till they were fine, then mixed them with a little bit of flour to make bread.

The bread was hard and tasted terrible, but Nettie was hungry. She ate all her share. Mama fed Frieda a piece she had soaked in milk. It looked like porridge. Frieda ate it eagerly. Nettie wanted to try her own bread soaked in milk – it looked much better than the bread she was eating – but there wasn't enough milk.

They didn't have coffee anymore. Sometimes Mama roasted grain and made prips. Papa said it was just as good as coffee. After making the drink, Mama took the grain that was left and mixed it into the bread. Nettie tried to decide if it was better than the bread made with thistles.

Sara saw the expression on Nettie's face. "I've heard of people putting garden soil in their bread," she said.

"Dirt!" said Nettie. "How can they?"

"People do what they need to do," said Mama. "I hope I don't need to put soil in the bread."

Nothing they ate was the same as it used to be. The potatoes were gone. The ham from Gerhard Funk didn't last long. There were no eggs.

"We have to eat the hens, Mama," said Sara.

"No, we'll keep them. They'll lay eggs again in the spring."

"No, they won't," said Sara. Mama stared at Sara. She wasn't used to anyone saying no to her. "They won't lay eggs in the spring because there is nothing to feed them. Without food, they will die. Even if we feed them all winter, they won't lay eggs in the spring."

Mama plopped down in a chair and stared at Sara. "What do you mean?"

"There used to be fourteen hens," said Sara. "Now there are eight. Maybe they died of starvation. Maybe foxes ate them. I think someone stole them."

"People are hungry," said Mama.

"If we don't eat them, someone else will," said Sara.

"You're probably right," said Mama. She heard Frieda cry from the bedroom. "Go get Frieda, Nettie. I must feed her." As Nettie left the room, Mama sighed. "We will make chicken soup every Saturday till the hens are gone," she said. "I hope we can get new chicks in the spring."

The only time they ate bread that tasted like bread used to taste was when Liese came to visit. Peter's parents had buried boxes of grain during the Terror. Now they had flour to make into bread whenever they were hungry. When Liese came, she usually brought a small loaf of bread or some noodle soup. Nettie wished she would come more often.

Nettie thought about this bread one afternoon when she was supposed to be thinking about Russian words. Papa said Nettie must study even though there was no school. It was hard to translate difficult Russian words when all she could think about was bread. Heavy, filling, almost-black rye bread. Fluffy, white, light-as-the-air *tweiback*. She even longed for the dry, roasted buns that she used to eat anytime she felt hungry.

The vision of bread disappeared when Mama interrupted her. "It's not so cold out today," Mama said. "I want you to go with Sara to the fields. See if you can find any small potatoes that the harvesters missed. No matter how small, we can still eat them. Collect feed for Daisy too. If you see any firewood, bring it back as well."

"We might as well be horses if we're to carry so much," Nettie muttered as she and Sara set out. It was hard to be cheerful when her stomach was hungry and she was always cold. Only while Mama made bread did the house get properly warm. There was not enough fuel to keep the stove hot all the time.

Usually they burned blocks of dried animal manure in the stove. Sometimes they twisted straw into tight bundles and burned it. There were few manure blocks left and no straw. They'd already cut many of the bushes around the house to burn, but they couldn't cut them all. Nor could they cut down the fruit trees without permission. They didn't own the schoolyard.

"We won't have much to carry," said Sara. "The grass and sticks have been picked so many times, there'll be nothing left. Next time we'll have to go much further from home."

Today, though, they went to the community garden and wandered up and down the patches. Most people picked their potatoes as carefully as the Pauls family. There were no small potatoes anywhere. Nettie shivered in her too-small coat, rubbing her hands together to warm them.

Wait, what could she see there? It didn't quite look like a pebble.

It was a potato; tiny, yes, but still a potato. Nettie saw another nearby. Sara found some too. They searched the whole area carefully and eventually had enough for two meals.

Nettie laughed as she looked at the tiny potatoes in her basket. "This will be so good," she said. "I can't wait till Mama sees them."

"Well, now. Look what you found."

Nettie looked up. A big man with a long, bushy beard stood in front of her. Nettie had seen him before, around the village and at church, but didn't know his name. He reached out and took the basket from her hands. "I see you picked these potatoes for me. I knew we had left some when we harvested. Much appreciated, young ladies. Here's something for your troubles." He reached into his pocket and pulled out a small coin.

"No," cried Nettie, reaching for the basket. "Those are ours."

"This is my garden," the man said. "So these must be my potatoes."

Nettie looked at Sara and Sara looked at Nettie. Nettie could feel the tears pricking at her eyes. She didn't care if it was rude; she turned her back on the man and started walking back the way they'd come.

"It's our basket," said Sara.

Nettie heard the man laugh but didn't watch to see what he did. Probably poured the potatoes into his hat or his pockets, or maybe he thought he could buy the basket for a coin too.

They could see three or four people off in the distance, probably looking for feed or fuel too, but there was no one close enough to hear them.

Sara reached out and took Nettie's hand. "It's okay, Nettie," she said. "God will give us food to eat."

They went into the bush to find a few twigs and a bit of dried grass and weeds. Back at the house, Mama had made soup thickened with ground corn cobs. Nettie tried not to listen while Sara told her parents what had happened. She particularly did not listen when Sara told them who the man was. She did not want to hate anyone, but oh, those potatoes would have tasted so good.

The next day Nettie saw Abram leave early in the morning. He didn't return at lunchtime, but in the middle of the afternoon he walked into the house.

"Abram," exclaimed Mama. "Where were you?"

A tiny smile played at the corners of Abram's mouth. "I've been out hunting," he said. "I brought something home for you."

Only then did Nettie notice his right arm behind his back. With a look of triumph, he held out two small brown animals hanging from a string. "Hedgehogs," said Abram.

"Supper!" said Mama. "You skin them. I'll fry them in drippings."

It was the best meal they'd had in days.

CHAPTER 25

January 15, 1922. We aren't the only hungry people. We were eating bread last night with only prips to go with it, when someone knocked at the door. There was a man there, so thin I don't know how he walked. "Bread for my children," he said in Ukrainian. "I need bread for my children." Mama invited him in, then took the bread that was left and gave it to him. "I couldn't eat if I didn't share," she said. People are eating anything they can find. Jacob told me people ate an animal they found dead in the field. It made them sick and a woman died.

Promises of food from America encouraged the village for months, but something always delayed it. Nettie wondered if it was all a lie and that really there was no food. Then one day in March it happened.

A wagon drove into the town loaded with bags of flour and boxes containing she didn't know what.

"The food has come," cried Nettie. "The food has come." The whole family gathered around the window that faced the street, watching as the wagon drove into the mill. Mama grabbed her shawl and hurried out. Nettie saw her talk to some of the men gathered around the mill, then she turned and headed down the street.

The group of men around the mill shrank as some of them went into the mill, then grew as more gathered. They seemed to be all talking at once, gesturing with their arms.

After a while, the wagon came out empty. Most of the men drifted away. Nettie's family lost interest too, leaving her alone at the window. She watched as all the men left except two. They stayed at the mill, sometimes walking around in front, sometimes leaning against the wall, sometimes talking.

"They're guarding the mill," Nettie said with sudden realization. Papa heard her. He got up slowly from his favourite spot by the stove and came over to see.

"Who are they guarding it from?" asked Nettie as she watched the men. "Makhno hasn't come back, has he?" Though it was many months since anarchists had visited the village, the thought still made Nettie's stomach clench.

"No," said Papa. "They are guarding it from hungry people."

Nettie nodded. There were stories of people going into someone's house, taking bread or coffee and once even a jar of soup. There were people who knocked at the door begging, other people who lay in the streets too weak to move. She understood how being hungry could turn anyone into a thief.

When Mama returned she was smiling. "Abram," she said to her husband. "They're opening a kitchen. It's in the old machinery factory. We're going to make soup and bread to feed the people. The food comes from Mennonites in North America."

"Good," said Papa. "That is very good."

"I will help cook," Mama went on. "Sara too. Nettie, you will have to stay and care for Frieda. You can come at noon each day and get some food."

"What about Papa and Abram? Do I bring food back for them?"

"There isn't enough to feed everyone." Mama's eyes were worried. "They are feeding children first, then women, men only if there is extra. Right now they don't think there is extra. We'll share our food with them. Sara and I are allowed more because we're working. It will be enough."

"When does it start?" asked Nettie. "When do we get the food?"

"Tomorrow," said Mama. "They have to get the kitchen ready. Tomorrow we make buns, the next day they should be ready for us to make soup."

It would be more than they had now, thought Nettie. Her mouth watered at the thought of filling soup and bread made of real flour instead of thistles.

Thank you, God, for the kind people who knew we were hungry.

Mama and Sara went early the next morning to prepare the food. Nettie played with Frieda and sang to her. The morning dragged on. She couldn't wait until twelve. A few minutes before, she asked Abram if he would watch Frieda and, not waiting for an answer, rushed out of the house.

She was not the only person to come early. The unused factory where they were making the food was surrounded by a crowd. Nettie was surprised to see many, many people she didn't know. They were not just Mennonites, but people from the Ukrainian villages nearby, and some she thought must be from the Lutheran villages. Would there be enough food for so many people?

There were tables and benches set up inside where people could sit, but Nettie took her buns back home with her. There was one each for her and Frieda, and another that was Mama's. Mama would share Sara's at the kitchen.

The buns were big – bigger than the *tweiback* Mama used to make. They were white and fluffy and warm in her hands. Nettie held them close to her face as she walked so she could smell the wonderful yeasty aroma. She noticed a spot on one where the crust was cracked. She broke a piece of it away. It was just a taste on the tip of her tongue, but it was so good she started walking faster.

At home she carefully cut each bun into halves, and then halves again. Each person had three quarters to eat. Frieda had never eaten such good food. She was so young, Nettie thought, she probably thought bread was supposed to be made from thistles. Abram didn't want to eat his. "I can't take your food," he said. "I'm doing nothing. I don't deserve this."

"Then do something," said Nettie. "Men are taking turns guarding the flour in the mill so no one steals it. You could do that too."

"I guess I could," said Abram. He lifted his cup to his mouth. When he set it down he bit into one of the pieces of bun.

"I had forgotten how good it could taste," he said, his voice so quiet Nettie barely heard.

April 15, 1922. Spring has come. We have planted our garden but there were so few seeds. Mama has heard there is a wagon filled with clothes coming to Gruenfeld. I hope she is right. People are wearing clothes they once would have used for rags.

"I'm going to learn to drive a tractor," Jacob announced when he came home one Sunday. "We'll take turns using it." Nettie could see that he was already considering himself one of the farmers, even though he was just a hired man.

"Where do you find a tractor?" asked Abram.

"Mennonites in North America are sending them," said Jacob. "They know about our horses being gone, so they're sending a whole ship full of tractors."

"I thought you liked horses," said Nettie.

"I do, but there aren't enough left," said Jacob. "I've never used a tractor. This is exciting."

Nettie shook her head. "I hope it rains."

Nettie wasn't a farmer, but two summers without rain had shown her that nothing grew without rain.

Jacob's cheerful smile dimmed a bit. "Without rain, it doesn't matter whether we plant the crops or not."

"But is there enough seed? I would have thought it was all ground up and eaten."

"A few farmers have some they hid away," said Jacob, "But most of it will come from the North Americans."

Nettie looked down at the shoes she was wearing. She had long since grown out of her old shoes, and there had been no money for new ones. With some mending, she had been able to wear one of Sara's old dresses, and Mama had used Nettie's outgrown, almost worn-out dress to make one for little Frieda, but shoes were not so easily come by. Many people had been wearing handmade wooden clogs because their shoes had been stolen and they had not been able to replace them. Now Nettie had shoes that were almost new and would fit her for a long time.

For Mama had been right. A wagon full of clothes had come to Gruenfeld. There were so many people needing clothes, however, that not everyone got everything they needed. Nettie would have liked a dress, but was grateful for shoes that didn't hurt her feet.

Papa had new clothes too. A black suit. It looked nothing like the suits he was used to wearing, but that didn't matter anymore. People wore anything that covered them and kept them warm. There was a time when no one Nettie knew would have worn clothes with patches on them. Now they had no choice. Nettie had even seen people wearing layers of clothes, hoping that by wearing two or three jackets, the holes would fall in different places and be as warm as wearing one good jacket.

Every day there was a reason to be thankful to the North American Mennonites. There were the buns and soup from the community kitchen. There were vegetable seeds. There were potatoes to plant in the garden.

It had been hard to see good food cut up and buried in the ground, but Nettie knew it was the only way to get new food. It had been hard for Mama too. She had saved the four biggest potatoes, peeled them carefully, and planted the peels. Then she had cooked the potatoes for supper. Nettie thought potatoes had never tasted better.

With the coming of spring an old chore had returned. Each day Nettie helped carry the washing-up water out to the garden. Sometimes as she poured the water over the rows, she talked to the seeds, encouraging them to grow, promising them more water the next day. Unfortunately, there was never enough water for all the rows.

CHAPTER 26

May 10, 1922. It rained just in time to save the potatoes. The grass is green again, so there is food for Daisy. I don't know how she lived on so little feed this winter. Mama traded some of her silk thread and was able to get five chicks. We eat dandelion greens now, and roots. Mama didn't think we had any relatives who would send us food, but she was wrong. One of Papa's cousins in America sent us a food parcel. It contained tea and canned milk and cocoa and rice. I liked the cocoa best, but everything was good. Liese is going to have another baby.

There was a meeting in the church. Papa and Mama both went, as well as Sara, but Nettie stayed home with little Frieda. Abram stayed home too, which surprised Nettie. She'd thought he would want to go.

Abram took his turn guarding the flour in the mill, and sometimes he found work with a farmer. The rest of the time he sat in the house, often reading Papa's books. It was good that Papa had been a teacher who had books, Nettie often thought. Otherwise what would he and Abram do?

Nettie played with Frieda, told her a story, and put her to bed. All the time, part of her mind was thinking about Mama and Papa and Sara at the meeting. They were talking about emigrating, she knew.

Nettie didn't know what to think about emigrating. She couldn't imagine travelling to the other side of the world. She couldn't imagine living anywhere but in Gruenfeld, in the teacherage, with people she knew all around her.

But if they emigrated to a country where her brothers wouldn't have to go in the army, where there would be food to eat every day, where bandits didn't ride through the villages shooting people...

That had to be a good thing, didn't it? And it would be an especially good thing if Liese and Peter came too.

Nettie tried to stay awake till her parents came home. Instead she fell asleep, and in her dreams she was on a big ship crossing the ocean to Canada. The ship was full of Mennonites, each of them carrying a pillowcase full of *tweiback*.

July 14, 1922. Our garden is full of vegetables. There is some food to eat, but we still have no money. The kitchens stopped making food for the village when the gardens started to grow. They gave each family flour so we could make our own bread till the new crop comes. The school is supposed to open again. There will be a new teacher. He is Russian. We will have to move one day, but not right away. Best news: I am an aunt. Liese had a baby. He is Peter Peters just like his father and his grandfather.

Nettie found so many more reasons to visit Liese now. Baby Peter was a rosy, happy baby who gurgled cheerfully when Nettie talked to him. Frieda, though little more than a baby herself, loved him as much as Nettie did. Whenever Mama let them, Nettie and Frieda walked down the street to Liese's house.

It was Sunday. Jacob and Abram were home for the day. Liese and Peter had come to visit. Everyone was sitting around the table visiting, everyone except Sara. She made the tea and put the bread on the table for *faspa*, singing quietly the whole time.

Sara always seemed to be singing, Nettie realized. She went to choir practice twice a week, and the rest of the time she sang while she worked. Jacob noticed too.

"What makes you sing so much, Sara?" Jacob asked. "Is there some special fellow in your choir that makes you want to sing?" Sara didn't answer Jacob, but she pressed her lips together and tossed her head. Nettie looked at her in amazement. Did Sara have a boyfriend? Was she going to get married too? She must watch carefully to see which young man Sara spoke to after church that evening. Then Papa spoke and Nettie forgot about Sara's boyfriend.

"I've filled out the forms," said Papa. Everyone looked at him.

"What forms, Papa?" asked Jacob.

"To emigrate," said Papa. "Russia has finally agreed to let some Mennonites leave. Landless Mennonites," he added. "People with no money, people who might be a burden on the country." Papa's voice sounded bitter, but then he shook his head and smiled faintly. "I never wanted to be a farmer anyway," he said. "And if I was, they wouldn't let me go."

"Will we all go, Papa?" asked Nettie. She looked around the table at her family. There were so many of them. "How can we pay for all of us to travel so far?"

"A big company in Canada is lending the money," said Papa. "The Mennonites in Canada are not rich enough, but this company is. It owns ships and trains. They will let us travel on credit. When we get to Canada, we will pay them back."

Jacob looked excited. Sara looked worried. Liese looked at Peter. Peter looked at his baby son. No one said anything.

Nettie couldn't stand the quiet. "How can we earn so much money, Papa? How will we pay them back?"

"We will work," said Papa. "The men must all promise to be farmers. Canada knows Mennonites are good farmers. That's why they will take us."

It didn't make sense, thought Nettie. Russia didn't want the farmers to leave, but Canada only wanted farmers.

"That's good," said Jacob. "I'll sign that paper. I want to be a farmer."

"You're just a boy," said Abram. "You can't be a farmer."

"What do you mean? I've been working since I was twelve. I can farm better than —"

"Jacob! Abram!" exclaimed Mama firmly. "Stop that, you are acting like children. You will both need to be farmers if we move to Canada. That is the only way we can leave Russia."

Abram looked angrily at Jacob, but neither of them spoke.

Nettie looked at Peter and Liese. "Are you going to come too?" she asked. "You don't have land."

Peter shook his head. "I don't think so, Nettie. I'll inherit my father's land. Maybe if things don't get better, we will come later."

Nettie looked at baby Peter. He waved a crust of bread in the air and laughed at Nettie. How could she leave them behind?

"There is just one problem," said Mama. Everyone turned to her. "Canada will only take healthy people. We must all be checked by doctors. If they say we aren't healthy, we can't go."

All eyes turned to Papa. Would the Canadians accept Papa?

CHAPTER 27

September 5, 1922. No one is going to Canada this year. They thought we would, but it is too late. Everything must wait till next year. Some people sold all their belongings, now they must wait till spring with no furniture or dishes. We didn't sell anything yet, but waiting is still hard. Jacob and Abram earned grain, so we have food to eat. Mama and Sara made more silk thread so we have something to trade in the market. School has begun, but I cannot go. If times were normal, I would go to Chortitza to the girls' school. I am reading Papa's books, even the Russian ones.

The days were long and the winter passed slowly. After waiting all summer, expecting every day to hear that it was time to leave for Canada, it wasn't easy settling down to another winter in Russia.

Sometimes Nettie wasn't certain she wanted to go to Canada, anyway. Things were better in Gruenfeld now. They hardly ever saw soldiers, there was food to eat, the government seemed to have stopped making laws that hurt the Mennonites. And Liese and Peter weren't moving to Canada.

Other times, when Nettie looked out the front window and saw Lena's house across the street, she remembered Makhno, the Red Army, the rules against speaking German, and the churches that were being closed in some parts of Russia. She wondered what had happened to Lena and whether her family had found a safe place to live. At those times, Nettie was ready to leave Russia too.

May 15, 1923. We have paid the fees for our passports and our names are on the list. The government changes its mind many times, but we pray that they will let us go this time. The name of our country has even changed. We don't live in Ukraine or even Russia. Since December, we have been living in the Union of Soviet Socialist Republics. We hear that the leader, Lenin, has had a severe stroke. Taking his place is a man whom many people fear. His name is Josef Stalin.

"Can't we take anything with us to Canada?" Nettie asked Mama. She saw people selling their belongings in the market. "We'll need dishes and chairs when we get across the ocean, won't we?"

"Yes, we'll need them, but we can't take them with us. We're only allowed to bring personal things like clothes. We aren't paying full fare to be able to take many trunks full of belongings. We can just take what we can carry."

"Are we going to sell our beds in the market?" Nettie definitely didn't want to sell her bed in the market. People would come and look at it, and maybe say it was not good enough and walk away. She would rather chop it up and burn it.

She knew people who had done that during the famine. They burned their furniture to keep warm. Mama and Papa only burned two pieces of furniture, an old table and a broken chair. They could have stayed warmer by burning more, but Mama said no. Now they had to sell it all anyway.

"We're going to sell all our furniture at once," said Mama, interrupting Nettie's thoughts as she looked around the room at all the furniture. "There's a man from another village who buys all the furniture in the house. He's coming this week. He will pay us now, then get the furniture when we leave."

Nettie was relieved that they wouldn't have to haul things to market. Even better, they would still have furniture till the day they left. Not like those families who sold everything last summer.

The man was coming on Thursday. On Wednesday, Mama took her best quilt and laid it on the table. Nettie watched from the doorway. Liese and Peter watched too, as Papa lifted the Kroeger clock off the wall and stilled the pendulum. Carefully, he laid it on the quilt.

Just as carefully, Mama wrapped the quilt around it. Her hand resting on the quilt, she smiled tremulously at Liese and Peter. "This is for you. Your grandparents gave your papa and me this clock for a wedding gift." Her voice was barely audible. "And now I want you to have it. One day, if...when you come to Canada, I hope you can bring it with you."

That night before they went to bed, Nettie saw Papa move towards the clock, to wind it. Partway there he stopped, and his hands dropped to his side. It was very strange not to have the clock. It had always been there.

THE NEXT DAY the man came to buy the contents of their house. Mama invited him in. Papa got up from the bench by the stove and walked around with the man. Nettie and Frieda shrank back against the wall as he looked over the furniture and peered into the cupboards. "Good quilts," he said once, but Mama protested.

"No," she said. "We need to take the quilts with us for the train."

The man made a note in his little book and glanced over the dishes in the cupboards. Finally he closed his little book. "I will give you thirty million rubles," he said. "And not one ruble more."

Thirty million. It sounded like a huge number, but Nettie knew thirty million rubles didn't buy much at all. Before the troubles it had been different. When Liese was married, thirty million rubles would have meant they were rich. They could have paid for their seats on the train, and the best ship across the ocean. Nettie looked anxiously at her father. How much would it buy now? Would it be enough to get them out of Russia? They had to pay for the train trip to the border.

"Sixty million," said Abram Pauls firmly. "Sixty million."

"Thirty million," said the man. He pulled up a chair and sat down at the table, placing his notebook on the table before him. "Many people are leaving. There is no market for dishes. Everyone has furniture. I've bought the contents of five houses already this week."

"Sixty million. People in Chortitza burned their furniture to keep warm. The bandits broke many dishes."

"Thirty million. The people in Chortitza have no money to buy furniture and dishes."

Frieda pulled at Nettie's hand. Nettie glanced down at her little sister. They weren't needed here. The two of them quietly slipped out the door. Nettie was sure no one saw them go. Just as she closed the door, Nettie heard her papa's voice.

"Sixty million," he said. Nettie didn't hear the rest.

There was so much to do to get ready to leave. Canada had said they would take the Mennonites, but there were many rules.

Everyone must be healthy. That was one of the rules. How can everyone be healthy, Nettie wondered, when for so long there has not been enough food or enough doctors?

There were medical checks, with doctors and nurses in white clothes looking in their mouths and listening to their hearts. They signed the papers saying the Pauls family were all healthy. Papa stood very straight and walked out of the building with hardly a limp. Nettie followed him, unable to stop smiling. They had said Papa was healthy.

Another rule was about all the men being farmers.

"Papa has never been a farmer," said Nettie.

"He will have to learn," said Sara. She spoke coldly. Sara didn't sing as she worked anymore. It was because of her friend, the one Jacob had teased her about. He wasn't going to Canada. Nettie wondered if Sara wanted to stay in Russia with him.

"Thread this needle for me, Nettie," said Mama. She handed Nettie a needle and a long silk thread. Sara bent her head and sewed in silence.

She and Mama were sewing bags out of heavy cloth to carry their belongings to Canada. Nettie didn't have much to take.

When the time came for them to leave, Nettie packed her extra underwear, all of her aprons, her second dress, and her comb. She didn't pack her diary. It would travel in the pocket of her apron where she would always have it with her.

Jacob would soon be back with the horses and wagon they were borrowing. Peter and Liese were coming with them to the train, then Peter would bring the wagon back.

Sara filled pillowcases with roasted *tweiback*. Mama hastily dusted the house. She folded a towel and laid it on the table. Everything they didn't take belonged to the man who'd paid them fifty million rubles.

Nettie looked around the house. She would never see it again. Never again would she look out the window and see the mill across the road where she and Lena had played. Never again would she warm her back against the stove as she wrote in her diary. Never again would the family sit and eat *vereneki* at the wooden table or disagree over who should wash the dishes.

Never again would she… "Mama! My tea set from Aunt Nettie. I can't leave my tea set behind!"

"You have to," said Sara. "That Man already bought it."

"Not my tea set!" exclaimed Nettie. "He didn't buy my tea set, did he, Mama?" She hadn't played with the set in years, but it was still her most treasured possession. Not even Lena had had such a beautiful tea set.

Mama opened her mouth to speak. She looked from Nettie to Sara and back to Nettie again. She closed her mouth. Then, with a swish of her heavy skirt, she swung around and scooped the small teapot up from where it nestled with the matching cups.

"He bought the cups," she said, "But he didn't buy the pot." Taking the towel she'd just folded, she wrapped the lid in one end and rolled the teapot up in the rest. "Have you room in your bag?"

"Yes, yes, of course," said Nettie eagerly. She pulled clothes out of the bag, making room for the teapot in the centre where it wouldn't get bumped. Then she stuffed the clothing back inside, a handkerchief inside the teapot itself.

"Jacob here," cried Frieda, who'd been watching the door, her rag doll clutched in one arm. "Jacob here."

"Then let's go," said Sara briskly.

"No," said Papa. Everyone stopped moving and looked at him.

"No," repeated Papa. "First we pray."

When Jacob came in, he saw the whole family kneeling together in the front room with their heads bowed.

He joined them, quickly stuffing his cap into his pocket.

"Thank you, Father," said Papa in his slow, quiet, praying voice. "Thank you for bringing us through these difficult times."

Difficult times, thought Nettie. All the fear, all the hunger, all the anticipation. Difficult times.

"Thank you for the men who found a way for us to leave this country."

The men in America – no, not America, Nettie corrected herself. Canada. And the men in Moscow. Men who talked to the governments and persuaded them that it would be good for the Mennonites to leave Russia and go to Canada. And the men who decided to lend money to the Pauls family and all the other families who had no money of their own.

"Thank you for the train that will take us to Latvia, and the ship that will take us to Canada."

Nettie, who had never travelled further than Chortitza to see the circus, would ride on a train and a ship and travel halfway around the world.

"We pray for your blessing on this trip. We pray for health as we travel. We pray for those who will travel with us and those who will operate the train and the ship. We ask your blessing on all these things. In Jesus' Name, Amen."

"Amen," repeated each of the family.

"And now let us go, so we don't miss this train," said Mama. They all stood up. When Nettie looked at Mama, for all her hurry, she was taking time to blow her nose.

CHAPTER 28

Chortitza, Ukraine, July 2, 1923.

Nettie had never seen so many people in one place. Everywhere she looked, there were people walking or riding in wagons. There were groups of people in yards and standing on the roads. Nettie wondered if it would take longer to drive through Chortitza than it had to travel the distance from Gruenfeld.

"I'm hot," whined Frieda. "Where's the train?" Much of Frieda's hair had escaped from her stubby braids and was curling damply around her face.

"It's right there," said Nettie, pointing down the street. "See where the people are unloading the wagons."

"Good!" said Frieda. She leaned her head against Nettie. "I want to go home."

Nettie didn't know what to say. Part of her felt the same as Frieda; she wanted to go home too. But Nettie wasn't three. She knew they couldn't go home. They had no home anymore. Everything they owned was in the wagon with them.

Because of the crowds, Peter couldn't get as close to the train as he wished.

"We can carry everything from here," said Jacob. "There isn't much."

He was right, thought Nettie. There wasn't much. The biggest parcels they had were the pillowcases full of roasted *tweiback* and the pile of quilts. It wasn't long before Abram, Peter, and Jacob had all the Pauls' belongings transferred to one of the train cars.

Not everyone in the crowd was leaving. Many more were there to say goodbye. Nettie stood by the wagon, clutching Frieda's hand, watching the hugging, the kissing, the farewells.

Occasionally someone laughed, but more often she saw tears.

"Liese, my Liese," said Mama, holding Liese's hands. "How can I leave you here?"

"And how can I let you go?" replied Liese. Nettie watched her as she forced a smile. "I'll miss you so much."

"We're supposed to board the train now," interrupted Jacob. Nettie hugged Liese one last time, then gave little Peter a kiss. "Come to Canada," she whispered, then followed the rest of the family through the crowd to the train.

Jacob lifted Frieda into the car, then helped Nettie scramble in. She tugged her dress back into place. The train was made up of boxcars, each furnished with improvised wooden benches and shelves. Some of the men had built the benches the day before. Nettie recognized her own cloth bag in a jumble on one of the wide benches.

Nettie tried to wave goodbye from the doorway, but the pressure of more people climbing in prevented her. Shoved to the back of the car, she fought back tears. She couldn't leave without seeing Liese one more time.

She tried to wriggle forwards, but the people made a wall, thick and unbreakable. Everyone wanted to be able to see for just a little longer. She stood on her tiptoes, but it made no difference. She jumped, making herself taller for just a moment, but it was no help. She still couldn't see over the heads in front of her.

What could she do? She needed to see Liese one more time. She couldn't go halfway around the world without waving goodbye to her sister! She looked down longingly. There'd be room to crawl between their legs, she thought. If she were three, like Frieda, she would do it. At fourteen, though, it was out of the question.

Then Nettie felt herself being lifted by strong arms, up into the air, so her head almost touched the top of the train car. "Can you see her now?" asked Jacob. "Wave my cap to get her attention."

Gratefully Nettie removed the flat, peaked cap from Jacob's head. Leaning forward as far as she could, she waved it wildly. She could see Liese now, still standing by the wagon. Peter stood beside her, waving his hat too, looking straight at Nettie, little Peter in his arms. She saw him point her out to Liese, then Liese waved her kerchief, one more spot of colour in the sea of waving arms.

Someone outside pushed on the door to shut it, but the people inside stopped him. "Not yet, not yet," a man called, "We'll close it later." The train started moving with a lurch that sent people clutching each other for support. For an awful moment, Nettie thought that Jacob would drop her, but he steadied himself just in time.

Nettie kept waving until the crowd at the train station was out of her sight. Even then, after Jacob let her down, Nettie darted forward to the now almost-empty doorway, hoping for one last glimpse.

The train swayed as Nettie clutched at the door frame, peering around it. The people were too small to identify, but she could still see their fluttering hats. She waved again with Jacob's cap, hoping Liese could still see her...hoping Liese would know who was waving. Then she felt an arm from behind come around her shoulders, steadying her and hugging her at the same time.

"Come, little one." Her father spoke slowly. "You mustn't fall out the door." Reluctantly Nettie turned away and followed him.

They found space by Mama on the rough boards that were to be their seats in the daytime and their beds at night.

Nettie wiped the tears from her face, ashamed that she was crying. Then she noticed that even her parents' eyes were wet. Little Frieda looked from one to the other, puzzled. She's too young, thought Nettie. She doesn't understand.

Nettie glanced around the car. It was crowded with neighbours and friends from Gruenfeld, along with a few people Nettie didn't know. Jacob was sitting with Abram across from Nettie, but Sara, where was she? Nettie's eyes darted around anxiously till she caught sight of Sara seated with a friend at the end of the car.

Dust blew in through the large open doorway, so a couple of men got up and pulled the door shut. Suddenly, it was dark in the car, with just fingers of light from the cracks in the walls.

It was not a comfortable way to travel, Nettie decided, but much faster than the wagon. As her eyes grew accustomed to the dimness, Nettie scrambled to the wall of the train and looked through the cracks between the boards. The fields and villages went by so swiftly. People stopped their working and watched the train. Nettie wanted to wave, but what was the use? They couldn't see her through the cracks.

Nettie's parents leaned against the bedding, their faces tired. Nettie looked anxiously at her father. How was he doing? The doctors said he was healthy, but Nettie knew he wasn't, not really. Unless...can people make themselves well just by deciding? Nettie wondered. If anyone could, it would be Papa, she knew. She felt her chest swell with love as she looked at him.

It was because of Papa that they were on the train today. It was Papa who decided the Pauls family needed to go to Canada.

"They won't let us go," a woman said quietly to Mama. "They want my whole family to die. My husband and my son were both killed at Zagradowka. They had gone to bring my husband's parents to us where it was safer, but they were all killed. Only my sister-in-law was spared; she hid in the garden. But then she died of typhus. They won't let me go. They want my whole family dead."

Mama patted the woman's hand. "Do you have other children?" she asked gently.

Nettie saw the woman's eyes flicker to a man and a woman holding two small children close to them, their faces almost as fearful as that of the woman speaking. "Yes, my daughter Anna and her husband. But I fear for them too. Oh no, is the train stopping?"

"No, they're just pulling over to let another train pass," soothed Mama. "Why don't we sing?" she suggested. "You'll feel better if you sing." The woman shook her head, but Mama didn't seem to notice. She started to sing "Now Thank We All Our God," and nodded to Nettie. Nettie joined in on the second line, and so did a man sitting nearby, and then the woman sitting beside him, and then more people. As each new person joined in the hymn, the harmonies were more beautiful. By the time they reached the last verse, the car was filled with the singing. Nettie looked at the woman beside Mama. Tears were running down her face as she, too, sang.

"ONCE WE'RE THROUGH THE RED GATE, we'll be safe," Nettie heard a man say.

"The red gate?" said another. "What is that?"

"There's a big gate," said the first man. "It stands on both sides of the track and meets over the top. It marks the border between Latvia and Russia. When we go through the red gate, we are safe."

After that, whenever Nettie looked through the crack in the wall, she looked for the red gate.

CHAPTER 29

July 7, 1923. At Charkov we bathed in a bathhouse. Our clothes were disinfected and nurses gave us needles to keep us from getting sick. There have been babies born on the train, but none are in our car. A baby would be nice, unless it cried a lot. Frieda fusses, so we have to play with her and tell her stories. I am already tired of eating roasted tweiback. I am glad we have our samovar to make tea.

The first few days of the trip they ate ham. When that was gone, there was nothing but buns and tea. Nettie thought longingly of milk. If they were to be farmers in Canada, they would surely have a cow. It was something to look forward to. Some people bought food when the train stopped in a station, but Nettie's family didn't have money for that.

There will be good food in Canada, Nettie told herself. She took another bite of the crusty bun. Beside the track, for the length of the train, people were crouching on the ground eating their lunches, their eyes always watching for signs of soldiers.

July 12, 1923. We've been on the train for ten days. We thought we could never leave Russia because the train could not make it up one hill. Even with a second locomotive it could not. Finally, all the younger men got out and pushed and even some of the older ones. Then the train made it up the hill. Jacob laughed when he got back on the train. Even Abram looked happy that they had helped. I would have helped too, but Mama said no. Our next stop was Sebesch. They say it is the last Russian station. We bathed in the lake and washed our clothes. We will leave Russia clean. Afterwards an inspector looked at all our belongings. He didn't see my diary.

"We must be close to Latvia," Nettie whispered to Frieda. Frieda looked at her wonderingly.

"Latvia," she repeated.

"Then we will be out of Russia," explained Nettie. "The Russians won't be able to stop us leaving once we're in Latvia."

"Latvia," said Frieda again. "Latvia."

Nettie smiled and hugged Frieda. Frieda relaxed against her for a moment, then wiggled away. "Sara," she cried. "I want Sara."

Nettie smoothed out her apron and pulled her diary from her pocket. She looked at the small homemade book. The book Liese had given her. Would she ever see her sister again? Nettie wondered. She opened to the first page. She'd been seven years old when Liese had given her the book. So much had happened since then. She slowly turned the pages, noticing how her writing had improved, how the entries had grown longer.

The clickety-clack of the train on the track changed. It slowed. Nettie looked up.

"Why are we stopping?" cried the frightened woman, Anna's mother. Nettie scrambled across the boards to the crack in the wall. She couldn't see the red gate. She couldn't see anything but trees and grass.

Then the door of the train car was pushed open. She turned and saw a soldier, dark against the brightness.

"Bring everything out of the cars," the soldier shouted. "Everyone stand beside your belongings. We must make sure you're not stealing anything from Russia. Take out those boards too. They are Russian boards."

Boards? thought Nettie. What did he mean? Was he talking about the benches and shelves? They weren't Russian. The Mennonites had built them themselves.

But the soldier *was* talking about those boards. Nettie watched as they were all dragged out. Then everyone's luggage was inspected.

"You can't take that," she heard a soldier say. She looked in the direction of the voice and saw someone giving a book to the Russians. A book! Nettie thought indignantly. People had brought hardly anything, yet these soldiers thought they had too much. Her hand went protectively to her pocket. Would they want her diary? Perhaps they would think she'd said things about the government in it.

When they got to the Pauls family, they searched rudely through each of the cloth bags that Mama had made. One of them glanced at Nettie's teapot, but he just tossed it back on the clothes without comment, then moved on to another bag. They didn't take any of their belongings away. Nettie wasn't surprised. Anything of value had been sold. All they had left were a few clothes and their bedding.

When the soldiers finished searching through the luggage, they waved to everyone to get back on the train. Nettie ran to pick up Frieda, who had wandered off. "It's time to go," she whispered to her little sister. "It's time to get back on the train."

Now there were no benches to sit on, nowhere to store their bags and boxes of belongings. As much as possible was piled along the walls, with people sitting on the piles as best they could.

Nettie turned and looked through the cracks in the side of the car. It was windy and dust blew in her eyes. She closed them partway, squinting through her lashes, peering towards the front of the train. When the track ran straight, there wasn't much to see, but occasionally the track curved and Nettie could see the front of the train ahead of them.

What could she see in the distance? Something tall and red.

She turned to Jacob, but someone else had been watching too.

"The red gate! The red gate! I can see it!"

Now everyone peered through the cracks in the walls. Cheers went up. Someone started singing, but before other voices could join in, Nettie felt the train slow down. Slower, slower, the train came to a halt. The cheers stopped. The singing died away.

All around her, people were praying. Some with their eyes closed, faces still, others moving their lips, but with no sound coming out. A few people prayed out loud.

Nettie reached out and took her father's hand. He looked down at her and smiled. "It will be fine," he said quietly. "God did not bring us so far to leave us in Russia."

As he spoke, the train started moving again. It gathered speed, hurrying on towards the red gate. The red gate and freedom.

Nettie, Abram, Papa, Mama – even Frieda, who had no idea what she was looking at – everyone was looking out the cracks to see when the train went through the gate.

The train passed through the tall poles of the gate. Nettie turned from the crack and looked around the car. So many people with tears running down their faces, so many smiles through the tears.

Papa reached out his good arm and put it around Nettie. Stretching it further he reached past her towards Jacob. On Papa's other side, Mama put one arm around him, and stretched her other arm to Abram. Nettie looked up to see that Sara had left her friends and was weaving around the people and belongings towards them. Frieda, perched on Mama's lap, was completely surrounded by her family.

It's a circle of love, thought Nettie. Mama and Papa, Abram and Sara and Jacob, Frieda and me. We're together. We made it out of Russia.

There's a whole new world out there that we've never seen. We've been through so much, she thought. We can make a good life in the new world. The new world of peace and freedom.

EPILOGUE

" And then you came here," said Lisa. "If you hadn't left Russia, I wouldn't be in Canada."

"Almost everyone who is here came from somewhere else," said Grandma Nettie. "North America is full of the descendents of people who were brave enough to leave their homes and move far away."

"And no one could be sure that things would be better in their new homes."

"We were full of hopes and dreams," said Nettie. "That's what brought us here. Hopes and dreams."

"And the train and the ship," said Lisa practically. "That must have been exciting."

"Riding on the train in Russia was not much fun," said Nettie. "Except, of course, that it took us out of Russia. To cross the ocean, we travelled on a ship. It was a big one, an ocean liner, called the Empress of France."

"What do you remember about the ship?"

"The food," said Nettie. "The food was wonderful. There was bread, white bread, of course, and fruits and puddings. There must have been meat and vegetables too. Most of it was unlike anything I'd ever tasted."

"And so different from what you ate during the famine."

Nettie nodded. "We travelled third class. We were supposed to stay on our own deck." She paused.

"But you didn't," Lisa guessed.

"Well, no," Nettie admitted. "It was probably the only time I would ever be on a ship. I wanted to see everything. It went very fast. I travelled with Jacob and Sara. We crossed the ocean in about a week. The ship Abram, Frieda, and my parents took was much slower. It was called the Bruton and took about three weeks. We docked in Quebec where we got on a train. A CPR train, of course. Canadian Pacific paid for our trip all the way from Russia to Saskatchewan."

"Canadian Pacific? That's a railway company, isn't it?"

"Yes, but they own ships and hotels too. A man from Rosthern, Saskatchewan, named David Toews persuaded them that Mennonites would be good to have in Canada. He guaranteed that if they paid our way here, we would pay all the money back. It took years, but we did it. We paid back every cent."

"And it was worth it?"

"Oh, yes. We had a good life here in Saskatchewan. I married your grandfather, we lived on this farm where you live now. We had six children – your father was the youngest one, of course – and now I have so many grandchildren. We've always had food to eat and we've never been afraid to go to bed at night.

"Yes, it was worth it. The Soviet government, they let twenty thousand Mennonites out and then they closed the borders. It was sad times for the people who stayed. Liese and Peter, they never did get out of Russia. We were the fortunate ones."

Nettie gazed off into the distance. Lisa watched her, knowing she was remembering the past.

"My father made sure we came," she said after a while. "It was the best thing he ever did for us. He brought us to Canada."

After a moment, Nettie reached into her apron pocket and brought out the diary, worn and ragged, its heavy cardboard cover cracked and stained. She held it out to Lisa, who took it carefully in her hands.

"I want you to have this now," Nettie said, "so you'll always remember."

AUTHOR'S NOTES

THE NOVEL YOU JUST READ is based on the life of Nettie Pauls Dueck, my mother-in-law. The main details are true to her life, but the body of the story is from my imagination, inspired by the stories she told me. Though she's forgotten many things, on one point her memory is firm. It was her ailing father who was determined to bring his family to Canada, and well into her nineties, Nettie is still grateful for that.

I have strived to make the story true to the times. The Russian Revolution really happened, the different political leaders mentioned were real people. There was a terrible famine that took the lives of hundreds of thousands of people. And twenty thousand Mennonites were given freedom when Canada welcomed them to come as farmers.

There are many books written about this period of history. Details from some of those books have found their way into these pages. For example, Lena's stories of the bandits breaking the china cabinet and dropping burning matches around her house were inspired by similar happenings recorded in *Russian Dance of Death*. Tina's story of the broken fruit jars came from the same source. Anyone wanting to know more than I could tell here might like to read one of these other books. The best choice for young readers is *Days of Terror* by Barbara Smucker. You can probably find it in your school library. For those who want to dig deeper, I have included a partial bibliography of the many books I read in preparation for writing this story.

GLOSSARY

Anarchists: People who don't believe in governments. Nestor Makhno led a large group of bandits in terrorizing the Mennonites, Jews, and other ethnic groups in Russia. They were able to do so much damage because of the long period when there was no government controlling what is now Ukraine.

Bolsheviks: The Communists in Russia, led by Lenin, who overthrew the government in November, 1917. Principles of Communism said that all people were equal, and no one should be more important than anyone else. No one was allowed to own property, so all business should benefit everyone equally. In practice, however, the leaders of the party did have more power, and when people didn't benefit personally from the work they did, they did not want to work.

Czar: The czar was the leader of Russia before the Revolution. Like kings or queens, he was an unelected leader who inherited his position. The last czar of Russia was Nicholas. Nicholas and most of his family were murdered by the Communists in July, 1918, a year and a half after he gave up his position as czar.

Emigration: When people move away from a country to take up residence somewhere else.

Faspa: Simple afternoon meal, often consisting of *tweiback*, cheese, jam, and cake.

Gruenfeld: Mennonites often chose descriptive names for their villages. Gruenfeld is the German word for Green Field. There were two Gruenfelds in Ukraine, each in a different colony.

Immigration: When people move to a different country. There were over 20,000 Mennonite immigrants to Canada in the 1920s.

Kommerz Schule: This was the business school that Abram attended when he finished the middle school. It was not exactly like our high schools, but it was still necessary for Abram to finish this school before he could go on to University.

Mennonites: The Mennonites originated in the Netherlands in the early fifteen hundreds when a priest named Menno Simons became convinced that what he was learning and teaching did not match what he read in the Bible. He and his followers left the Roman Catholic Church to start their own church, which included belief in pacifism and adult baptism. Persecuted for their beliefs, they moved to Poland, where they were allowed to worship in the way they believed right. In 1772, the area of Poland they lived in became part of Prussia. At that point, they lost their military exemption. They had become such successful farmers that in 1786 Catherine the Great of Russia invited some of them to farm in Ukraine. She promised them freedom to worship and to educate their children in their own way, as well as freedom from military service and the right to speak their own language. All of these rights were taken away over a period of years. Mennonites began leaving Russia in 1874 after the government said the children had to learn Russian in school.

Moos: Fruit soup. The most common *moos* was made from dried fruit, particularly plums, *pluma moos*. It was also made from many different fresh fruits when they were in season.

Plautz: Yeast dough patted into a pan, covered with sliced fruit, then baked with crumbs or sugar topping.

Plautdietsch: Low German, a language that has only recently become a written language. When Nettie was a child, it was only a spoken language.

Poltaovent: Party held the evening before a wedding. It was the time when gifts were exchanged and a humorous program was presented.

Prips: Coffee substitute made from grain.

Sabre: A sword. Frequently carried by the anarchists who were terrorizing the Mennonites.

Schloapbenjk: A sleeping bench. Common in Mennonite homes, it was a bench in the daytime, but when the lid was opened it became a bed for the night.

Tweiback: Low German for "two buns." It is a white bun with a second smaller bun pressed into the top. It takes skill to make them so the second bun doesn't fall off in baking. Any left after a couple of days were slowly roasted in the oven so they wouldn't spoil.

Vereneki: Small circles of dough filled with cottage cheese, potato, or fruit, then folded over, sealed, and boiled. Often called perogies.

Verst: Russian measurement. One verst is similar to one kilometre.

CHRONOLOGY OF
SOME IMPORTANT EVENTS

August, 1914: Beginning of First World War

November 3, 1914: Russian decree prohibits public use of German language.

February–March, 1917: Czar resigns and provisional government is put in place.

November 7–9, 1917: Bolsheviks take control of Petrograd and begin their period of power over Russia.

December 15, 1917: Russians sign armistice with Germany, ending their involvement in the First World War.

March 3, 1918: Treaty of Brest-Litovsk gives Ukraine independence.

April, 1918: German troops move into Ukraine.

November 11, 1918: End of First World War, followed by retreat of German troops from Ukraine.

November, 1920: Red Army defeats Whites, gaining control of Ukraine, followed by attacks on the Makhnovites. Makhno himself escapes to Paris.

1921 to 1922: Severe famine throughout Russia.

March, 1922: American relief supplies reach Mennonite colonies.

June 22, 1923: First group of emigrants leave Chortitza for Canada.

BIBLIOGRAPHY

Epp, Frank: *Mennonite Exodus.* Published for Canadian Mennonite Relief and Immigration Council by D.W. Friesen and Sons Ltd., Altona, Manitoba, 1976.

Hiebert, P.C.: *Feeding the Hungry – Russian Famine 1919-1925.* Mennonite Central Committee, Scottdale, Pa., 1929.

Lohrenz, Gerhard: *The Fateful Years 1913-1923.* The Christian Press, Winnipeg, Manitoba.

Lohrenz, Gerhard: *Storm Tossed, a personal story of a Canadian Mennonite from Russia.* The Christian Press, Ltd., Winnipeg, Manitoba, 1976.

Neufeld, Dietrich: *Russian Dance of Death.* Herald Press, Scottdale, Pa., 1978.

Smucker, Barbara: *Days of Terror.* Clarke, Irwin & Co., 1979.

ACKNOWLEDGEMENTS

THANK YOU TO NETTIE PAULS DUECK for being my inspiration. Your many stories begged to be retold and remembered. Thank you to Margareta Pauls Fleuter. Your amazing memory for the details of Russian Mennonite life has never let me down. Thank you for encouraging me, for lending me your books, and for reading the manuscript. And to my family: thank you for listening to years of Mennonite stories and patiently standing by me when the words flowed and when they didn't.

Thank you to Barbara Sapergia for seeing things I couldn't see, to Linda Aksomitis for reading the manuscript and offering valuable advice, to the Saskatchewan Children's Writers Round Robin for being there and reminding me that writers write, and to the Canada Council for the Arts for confirming my faith in the story by awarding me a grant.

ABOUT THE AUTHOR

ADELE DUECK has published one other book for children, *Anywhere But Here* (1996), which was a finalist for the Silver Birch Award in Ontario, and for Manitoba's Young Reader's Choice Award. Her fiction has appeared in several children's anthologies, while magazine articles have been published in *Western People, Farm Woman, Grainews,* and *Canadian Living.*

Originally from the Outlook area, Adele Dueck lived in Drake, Lanigan, and Saskatoon before returning to nearby Lucky Lake, where she farms with her family.

FROM MANY PEOPLES

Coteau Books began to develop the *From Many Peoples* series of novels for young readers over a year ago, as a celebration of Saskatchewan's Centennial. We looked for stories that would illuminate life in the province from the viewpoints of young people from different cultural groups and we're delighted with the stories we found.

We're especially happy with the unique partnership we have been able to form with the LaVonne Black Memorial Fund in support of *From Many Peoples*. The Fund was looking for projects it could support to honour a woman who had a strong interest in children and their education, and decided that the series was a good choice. With their help, we are able to provide free books to every school in the province, tour the authors across the province, and develop additional materials to support schools in using *From Many Peoples* titles.

This partnership will bring terrific stories to young readers all over Saskatchewan, honour LaVonne Black and her dedication to the children of this province, and help us celebrate Saskatchewan's Centennial. Thank you to everyone involved.

Nik Burton
Managing Editor, Coteau Books

LAVONNE BLACK

My sister LaVonne was born in Oxbow, Saskatchewan, and grew up on a small ranch near Northgate. She spent a lot of time riding horses and always had a dog or a cat in her life. LaVonne's favourite holiday was Christmas. She loved to sing carols and spoil children with gifts. People were of genuine interest to her. She didn't care what you did for a living, or how much money you made. What she did care about was learning as much about you as she could in the time she had with you.

We are proud of our LaVonne, a farm girl who started school in a one-room schoolhouse and later presented a case to the Supreme Court of Canada. Her work took her all over Saskatchewan, and she once said that she didn't know why some people felt they had to go other places, because there is so much beauty here. LaVonne's love and wisdom will always be with me. She taught me that what you give of yourself will be returned to you, and that you should love, play, and live with all your heart.

LaVonne felt very strongly about reading and education, and the LaVonne Black Memorial Fund and her family hope that you enjoy this series of books.

Trevor L. Black, little brother
Chair, LaVonne Black Memorial Fund

LaVonne Black was a tireless advocate for children in her years with the Saskatchewan School Boards Association. Her dedication, passion, and commitment were best summed up in a letter she wrote to boards of education one month before her death, when she announced her decision to retire:

"I thank the Association for providing me with twenty-three years of work and people that I loved. I was blessed to have all that amid an organization with a mission and values in which I believed. School trustees and the administrators who work for them are special people in their commitment, their integrity, and their caring. I was truly blessed and am extremely grateful for the opportunities and experiences I was given."

LaVonne was killed in a car accident on July 19, 2003. She is survived by her daughter, Jasmine, and her fiancé, Richard. We want so much to thank her for all she gave us. Our support for this book series, *From Many Peoples,* is one way to do this. Thank you to everyone who has donated to her Memorial Fund and made this project possible.

Executive, Staff, and member boards of
The Saskatchewan School Boards Association

Also available in the series

CHRISTMAS AT WAPOS BAY

by Jordan Wheeler & Dennis Jackson

At Christmas time in Northern Saskatch-ewan, three Cree children –
Talon, Raven, and T-Bear – visit their *Moshum's* (Grandfather's) cabin to
learn about traditional ways and experience a life-changing adventure.

ISBN: 978-1-55050-324-1 – $8.95

ADELINE'S DREAM

by Linda Aksomitis

Adeline has to struggle to make a place for herself when she comes to
Canada from Germany. Life in her new home is definitely dramatic, but by
Christmas time she starts to feel a sense of belonging in her new home.

ISBN: 978-1-55050-323-4 – $8.95

THE SECRET OF THE STONE HOUSE

by Judith Silverthorne

Twelve-year-old Emily Bradford travels back in time to
witness her ancestors pioneering in Saskatchewan and
discovers a secret that will help explore her family's roots in Scotland.

ISBN:978-1-55050-325-8 – $8.95

Available at fine bookstores everywhere.

Amazing Stories. Amazing Kids.

WWW.COTEAUBOOKS.COM